DANA CHRISTINE HARE

Red Flags & Roses

A Non-Monogamous Dark Romance Novel

First edition

ISBN: 9798874235093

This book was professionally typeset on Reedsy.
Find out more at reedsy.com

This book goes out to all the girls, gays, and theys that go absolutely feral for an unhinged and emotionally unavailable man.

Also a big thanks to my two partners in real life for pushing me to write this story.

TRIGGER WARNINGS

This book is a dark romance novel suitable for adults only. Please do not use this book as educational material on how to have sex, partake in the BDSM community, or healthy relationships. Please be advised that this novel contains themes and elements that may be disturbing or triggering to some readers. Discretion is advised. There is more smut than plot if you were expecting a traditional romance novel you will be disappointed.

The following list provides specific content warnings:

- Mature Content: This book contains explicit sexual scenes and strong language.
- Violence and Abuse: Scenes of physical, emotional, and/or sexual violence are depicted.
- Mental Health and Trauma: The story includes discussions and depictions of mental illness, trauma, and PTSD.
- Substance Use: Characters in this book engage in or are affected by the use of alcohol and drugs.
- Dark Themes: The narrative explores complex and dark emotional themes, including manipulation and power dynamics in relationships.
- Non-Consensual Acts: There are instances of non-

consensual sexual activities and dubious consent.
- Disturbing Imagery: Some scenes may include disturbing or graphic imagery.

Scenes include, but are not limited to, bullying, drug use, alcohol use, rape, consensual non consent, non-monogamy, choking, bondage, impact play, floggers, paddles, face slapping, sexual assault, violence, scenes of group sex, graphic sex, voyeurism, exhibitionism, sadism, masochism, orgasm denial, edging, pegging, anal, knife play, kidnapping. Reader discretion is strongly advised. If you feel that any of these themes might trigger a negative emotional or psychological response, please consider your well being before reading.

HELPFUL DEFINITIONS

- Polyamorous: To be polyamorous means to have open intimate or romantic relationships with more than one person at a time.
- Polycule: An umbrella term which describes a connected network of people and relationships, all of whom are in some way involved emotionally, sexually, or romantically with at least one other person within the polycule.
- Compersion: A form of joy in the joy of others. In the world of non monogamous relationships, it more specifically relates to the happiness someone finds in their partner seeking out and enjoying sexual and romantic intimacy with other people.
- Throuple: A relationship of three people all together.

PLAYLIST

- Taxi- The Maine
- Someone New- Hozier
- Piece Of Your Heart- Mayday Parade
- Swim- Chase Atlantic
- Gentleman- Gallant
- THE ONE YOU LOVED- The Plot In You
- love or chemistry- nothing,nowhere.
- Lavender Haze- Taylor Swift
- XO / The Host- The Weeknd
- Initiation- The Weeknd
- PILLOWTALK- ZAYN
- Peaches & Cream- Noah Davis
- Norman Fucking Rockwell- Lana Del Rey
- FUCK ABOUT IT- Waterparks, blackbear
- Heartbreak Feels So Good- Fall Out Boy
- Say Yes To Heaven- Lana Del Rey

Prologue

In the heart of a city where the nights whispered secrets and the days blurred into anonymity, there lived a woman named Callie. She was a canvas of stories, her tattoos that she was covered in were a tapestry of her soul's journey, adorning her from head to toe, each line and color a chapter of her life. At thirty years old, and five foot six, she carried herself with a confident grace, her curves an ode to the celebration of her body's journey through time and emotion. Callie had seen worlds within and beyond the confines of the conventional, her piercing blue eyes reflecting a life less ordinary.

Callie's heart and home were shared in an unconventional way, she was entwined in a polyamorous relationship with her husband, Jake, and their shared girlfriend, Alejandra. Jake, in his early thirties, had a presence so unassuming yet undeniable. A man of few words, he spoke a language of tender gestures and thoughtful silences. His simplicity was the perfect counterbalance to the vibrant complexity of Callie.

Alejandra, a curvy Latina beauty in her early twenties, was the fire that danced between them. Her laughter was a melody that filled their home, her spirit as warm and inviting as the sun. The dynamics of their throuple were like a carefully choreographed dance, each step, each pause, a testament to their shared understanding and respect.

Yet, amidst this harmonious existence, Callie felt a stirring in her soul, a whisper of desire for something, or someone, to add a new dimension to their lives. Her search was not born of discontent but of curiosity, a yearning to explore the vast landscapes of love and connection. She longed to find her perfect third partner that would meet the rest of her needs and sexual desires.

It was on one surprising night, that a chance encounter would turn the page to a new chapter in Callie's life. In the dim light of a popular club, where the music pulsed like a heartbeat and the shadows held secrets, Callie's gaze met a pair of eyes that seemed to see right through her inked armor, into the depths of her untold stories.

Those eyes belonged to someone whose presence immediately felt like a missing piece to an ever-evolving puzzle. In that moment, Callie knew that their lives were about to change, that the dance of their throuple was poised to welcome a new rhythm, a new harmony.

In the depths of her soul, Callie was a seeker—a woman unafraid to explore the depths of her desires, challenge the confines of conventional love, and paint her world with the vibrant colors of her chosen relationships. She stood at the intersection of bravery and vulnerability, her spirit unbound and her heart an open invitation to those willing to embrace the intricacies of her existence.

The world was not always kind to those who dared to defy its norms. Yet, in her heart, Callie believed in the power of love and love alone, and that is where our story begins.

Chapter 1: 8/12

It was Friday morning, and the weekend was off to an unusual flow compared to what was normal in our house of chaos. Jake was out of town for a few days on a work trip. He was sent off to the hustle and bustle of New York City and I was left at home with an insane feeling of jealousy and fear of missing out. Alejandra and I were doing our best to entertain each other despite getting photos every other hour from Jake of him sipping cocktails in swanky bars. He assured us it was a work trip, but it just seemed like an all inclusive paid for vacation truly. The only perk of Jake being gone was we didn't have to sleep three to our king sized bed and we unashamedly could watch our trash reality television shows all week.

The weekend upon us, Alejandra didn't want us to stay home and wallow in our jealousy of our lives being boring in comparison to Jake's fun NYC weekend. It was Friday after all, and the city was our oyster to do whatever we wanted. Girls night? Girls' night with us almost seemed dangerous. At least being together, both literally and relationship wise, we knew we couldn't get into too much trouble. An Uber there, an Uber home, already knowing we'd be leaving with each other. What could go wrong?

Alejandra and I decided to go all out if we were going to go out at all. Her idea was that without our shared male partner accompanying us, we could get all dressed up and dance the night away while letting single men at the club pay for our drinks all night. Admittedly, a good idea, harmless fun. She wore a tight hot pink body con dress, and continued to be on a bimbo Barbie pink theme with matching accessories. Adorned in dangle earrings that said "Slut" and a pink leather collar I had given her complete with a silver heart lock that I held the key to. She wore her favorite shiny white go-go boots, I was hoping she wouldn't complain about her feet hurting later. The look was completed with a sharp wing eyeliner.

I picked out a dress that complimented my girlfriend's look while still being unique to my own more alternative image. It was a subtle spring green colored dress with a midriff cutout and it was pink flower patterned. It was tight, revealing, and showed off all of my tattoos. I decided to be as extra as I possibly could be and wore a bleach blonde wig to channel a party energy for the night. As I put on the finishing touch of some pink lip gloss to my outfit, Alejandra hollered from downstairs about the Uber being three minutes away to take us to our destination.

In the pulsating heart of the club, The Social, amidst the rhythmic beats and swaying bodies, I immediately found myself caught in the kaleidoscope of lights and laughter. A gin and tonic in hand eased me into the evening. We chiseled out a section on the dance floor knowing that some friends were meeting up with us and planned on dancing the night away, losing ourselves in the thrill of the music. Alejandra's infectious smile mirrored my own as we reveled in this much-needed escape from the demands of reality. I was glad we got out for the night.

My gaze swept over the club, taking in the countless amount of faces lost in the music, the array of lights that painted everyone in hues of blues and purples. The Social was more than a club; it was a haven for those who lived and loved outside the lines. It was a place where we could be ourselves without the weight of judgment.

Alejandra's laughter filled the room with warmth and could be heard over the music. "Let's dance," she urged, her hand outstretched, an invitation to get lost in the rhythm.

Dancing with Alejandra was like being caught in a storm; it was exhilarating, wild, and freeing. She truly danced like nobody was watching, but everyone was. She just didn't care. As we danced, I could feel the gaze of others on us, a mixture of curiosity and desire, but in that moment, nothing mattered but the music. After all, I was dancing with the most gorgeous girl in the club.

The Social throbbed with life, each corner a vignette of human emotion and connection. My eyes often wandered, observing the intimate moments shared in the shadows, the laughter and conversations that filled the air. This was a world I understood, and understood well.

As the hours waned and the night eventually beckoned its farewell, our legs tired from dancing, and our bodies unable to handle more alcohol, Alejandra decided it was time to bid adieu to the vibrant chaos. She maneuvered through the crowd to find me as we inevitably got separated between friends, conversations, and trips to the bathroom and bar.

"Hey, let's head out, I am pretty ready to go, we should say goodbye to our friends though!" she insisted.

Stumbling tipsy toward the exit, my gaze momentarily drawn to an enigmatic figure leaning against the bar. It was him—

Benji, the local tattoo artist whose mere presence always set my heart racing. He worked at the shop I went to get my own art done at, but sheer anxiety and intimidation kept me from him. He had to know about me, but we never talked before. Something about him just screamed adventure in human form. His eyes held a spark of familiarity, as if we had shared a secret connection through fleeting glances when our paths had crossed previously.

I had previously admired him from afar, often imagining the stories behind the intricate designs that adorned his skin. Tonight, a surge of boldness coursed through my veins as I derailed from the path towards the exit and I made my way toward him, determination fueling each step. The gin was definitely overpowering any ounce of anxiety I had. I was on a mission.

"Hey," I said, my voice carrying a small hint of nerves as I approached him. "Didn't expect to see you here."

Benji turned, his gaze meeting mine with a curious sparkle. "Callie, right? Yeah, I like to pop in every now and then." His smile was magnetic, drawing me in with an irresistible charm that held me captive.

Our conversation flowed effortlessly, like we had been long time friends. The minutes stretched into moments that seemed to defy the passage of time. Alejandra picked up on queues and melted back into the crowd with our friends without speaking a word. I found myself drawn deeper into his world, hanging onto his every word, savoring the shared laughter and the secrets exchanged in hushed tones over the din of the club.

"Yea me and Em broke up a month ago, tonight is my first real night out since!" The revelation of his newfound single status sent a jolt of excitement coursing through me. I knew this was my chance, a moment to seize the opportunity fate had placed in my path.

As I glanced at my phone to check the time, the realization of my intention to leave hung in the air, but Benji's presence alone anchored me in place. Alejandra had texted me, "Just let me know when you're ready and I'll order the uber home, you seem distracted, I'll give you a minute."

Benji's lingering touch, the way he held my gaze, it made my heart race with a longing I just couldn't ignore.

With a subtle invitation in his eyes, I knew the night wasn't over. The question lingered in the air, —would I succeed in luring him back home with us? Would Alejandra be upset? We were about to risk it all and find out.

Before I could ask him to leave with me, he said "Hey, I'm here with my best friend Chad, I think he's on the patio having a smoke, wanna join me?" I felt myself getting sucked into staying a lot longer than I had anticipated just a few moments prior to running into him.

"Yeah, sure!" Benji took my hand and led me through the crowd of The Social to the back door. His fingers interlocked with mine and I succumbed to the feelings of butterflies in my chest.

Shockingly upon being on the back patio, Alejandra was with some of our friends just a hair away from Chad. She glanced at me, then at Benji, then back at me and winked before going back to the conversation she was having. Her wink was seemingly a sign of approval which helped me feel less rushed on leaving.

"Hey Callie, this is Chad, Chad this is Callie. I've been staying with him since the breakup with Em, we've been best friends since high school." I formally shook his hand and then took it upon myself in this moment of introductions to blend the groups. "It's lovely to meet you, I'm here with my girlfriend Alejandra, hey! Alejandra! Come here and meet some friends!" She approached us and one of our friends, Macy, followed her.

Alejandra didn't seem to be upset that we were still at the club despite her suggesting we leave just forty minutes prior. If anything it seemed that she rallied and had a second wind of energy. I felt myself losing the attention of Benji, maybe me being with my girlfriend turned him off assuming that I was monogamous and unavailable. After all that is the societal norm. I hated working into conversation that I was polyamorous to people who were uneducated about it. What's the easiest way to tell someone you're not single but available?

It was in that moment that Macy, very inebriated, pulled through and saved the moment. "Callie! I know you're here with Alejandra, but she's looking so good, do I have your consent to kiss her?"

"Of course!!" I said, Chad and Benji now looking at me with confusion as I just let someone else fully make out with my partner. "Oh we're polyamorous, Macy didn't have to ask but it was a nice gesture that she did. I have a husband too, but he's out of town this week." Chad and Benji were speechless. I decided fuck it, I wanted to be as brave as Macy with her liquid confidence. "Hey Chad, I know you're here with Benji, but with his consent as well, can I kiss your best friend?"

"Please! Wow, I've never seen such open and casual consent like this before, is this okay with your girlfriend too?" We looked back at Alejandra to clarify, but she was still tongue deep with Macy insinuating that yeah, us kissing other people was very okay. "Benji, may I then?" I asked him directly. He grabbed my face with both of his hands, leaned his body into mine, without a verbal yes, and then pushed me up against the brick wall and locked lips with me. He seemed to want that just as much as I did.

The first words after the kiss that slowed time came out quiet, creeping and slow from my mouth. Trying to invite someone back home from the club while being polyamorous and bringing my girlfriend home too wasn't the norm for most people. "Hey, so my girlfriend, well she was just about ready to go before I ran into you...would you want to come home with us? We were about to order an uber..."

"I drove tonight, but...yea, sure, why not." He tossed his keys to Chad and told him to take his car home. "I'm gonna uber back to Callie's with her and her girlfriend. I'll see you in the morning!" He was already so sure that he was staying the night. What thoughts were rushing through his head? Were they the same as mine? What was the rest of the night going to entail?"

We walked to the front of The Social as a unique little trio waiting on a 2014 Kia Soul to pick us up and bring us to the house. As we piled into the backseat of the Uber, the air felt electric. Alejandra's hand was warm in mine, her laughter floating like music. Beside me on the other side sat Benji, his arms folded casually, his easy smile mingling with the neon lights flashing through the window as we drove out of downtown.

"Callie, you sure this is cool?" Benji's voice, tinged with curiosity, brushed against my ear.

I glanced at Alejandra, gauging her comfort. "Absolutely. You have nothing to worry about, let's just enjoy the night."

The ride hummed with a strange energy—a blend of excitement and tension. The city lights streaked past us, casting shifting shadows on our faces, the lack of conversation was awkward aside from Benji just asking a lot of questions about polyamory, the Uber driver probably was equally confused listening in on us.

Benji leaned forward, "So, what's the plan once we're back?"

His question hung in the air, a weighty anticipation. "Well," I began, a hint of nervousness threading my words, "I thought we could just hang out. Maybe share some more drinks, chat?"

Alejandra nodded, her enthusiasm infectious. "Sounds fun! I'll probably share one more drink with you two and then head to bed and give you both your space!"

As we pulled up to the house, the atmosphere shifted. The threshold of my home suddenly felt like the gateway to a realm of possibilities. Opening the door, we stepped into a space that was a canvas of my life—filled with books, prints, an array of vinyl records, and strange mementos of adventures past. Benji's eyes traced the room, taking in the eclectic mix of decorations, while Alejandra made herself at home, kicking off her boots and settling onto the couch.

"Anyone want a nightcap?" I offered, eager to ease the transition from the vibrancy of the night to the intimacy of home.

Benji followed, his voice a quiet hum behind me. "Sure, what do you have?"

This was the first time he was at my house, a house designed for hosting. "Well, here's the bar!" I gestured towards a china hutch with over 4 dozen types of liquor and liqueur bottles. "We have just about everything, we host a lot of parties."

I ended up making simple dessert cocktails for us to end the night with, some vodka, white chocolate liqueur, and a bit of Kahlua, something impressive but simple. A nice nightcap to direct the evening into something else after one drink at home. Returning to the living room, I found Alejandra and

Benji engaged in an animated conversation, laughter bubbling between them.

Sinking into the couch, the next twenty minutes while we sipped cocktails unfolded like a delicate tapestry. Conversation flowed effortlessly, transcending into the topic of boundaries of conventional relationships, Benji learning quickly a lot of the intricacies of my lifestyle and relationships. Seemingly he was very chill about all of it.

I caught Benji stealing glances in Alejandra's direction, his admiration evident, I can't blame him, she's gorgeous. Her gaze lingered on Benji's tattooed arms, a silent appreciation.

Eventually, Alejandra stood up swallowing the last of her drink. "Well I bid the two of you adieu for the night. You guys have fun."

Her departure hung in the air, a pivot point in the evening. A charged silence enveloped the room, brimming with desires and uncertain paths. Benji and I exchanged a glance, curiosity lingering between us.

Benji was very settled on the couch, a quiet contemplation in his eyes. I inched closer to him, the distance between us now an invisible thread pulling taut. Our eyes met, the echoes of our shared moment at the bar flickering between us like a flame yearning to be kindled once more.

"Tonight's been…" Benji trailed off, his words dancing on the edge of something unspoken.

"Unexpected?" I offered my voice a soft echo in the room.

"Yeah, but in a good way," he admitted, his gaze locking with mine.

The silence between us hummed with a question, a hesitation laced with longing. I reached out, tracing the rim of my glass, searching for the courage to bridge the gap between us. "You

14

know, back at the bar..."

Before I could finish, Benji leaned in, his lips meeting mine in a gentle yet urgent embrace. The taste of alcohol lingered as our kiss deepened, the chemistry between us igniting into a flame that blurred the lines between friendship and something more.

I knew I couldn't expect too much, after all we were both a bit tipsy, he was newly single, and it was already 4 o'clock in the morning.

"So, I'm not like other girls. I can't take you back to my room, but we do have a guest room available for us to use, well, a red room of sorts." jokingly but generally serious. "My throuple has the boundary of respecting our bedroom as a sacred space, but we designed the red room guest room as a fun room for our external partners, I'm sure it might be a bit overwhelming for you and not the typical thing you expect from a Friday night drunken hook up."

I looked down at my phone, opening an app to turn all the fun lights on in the room before we walked in there together. I really wanted to make a lasting impression. Benji was just SO COOL and I wanted to feel like I was cool too and he wasn't completely out of my league. Guided by an unspoken understanding, we moved toward the bedroom, our footsteps echoing the crescendo of anticipation.

Center in the room, a queen sized canopy bed. One wall behind the headboard was velvet red curtains. The rest of the walls were black and precariously decorated with lude and nude art. The shelves on the walls were home to flickering flame less candles, a delicately placed metal cock cage, some leather cuffs, and various butt plugs and dildos just on display. The room was lit up with purple and red LED lights truly

15

setting a mood of the room for lust and passion. A spanking bench in the corner, floggers, paddles, and crops hanging from the bed

"So this is my red room." I said with reserve in my voice, I realized in that moment that this was a lot to throw at a person all at once. Benji looked stunned. Maybe this was too much. Kink isn't everyone's cup of tea. Should I have warned him?

"This is incredible Callie. I'm going to make you my pet tonight."

I nearly fainted. Clearly he was into kink. I was dying to be his pet. I giggled awkwardly to fill the silence and lowered myself down to a sitting position at the edge of the bed. He leaned over to kiss me, his burly hands at either side of me holding himself steady. He was pushing into me, just forcefully enough to scoot me further back on the mattress as he climbed on top of me.

"Can I take this off for you?" he subtly and politely asked while simultaneously just taking my dress off without giving me time to even answer. Lifting from the bottom right around my thighs the dress came off nice and easy over my head.

"Well now in comparison you look overdressed" I said in a bratty tone as I went for the button on his jeans, fidgeting with the zipper and my long acrylic nails as he pulled his black t-shirt up and over his head. His hands met mine around his waist shimmying the denim down his thighs revealing more and more of his tattoos the lower we went.

There we were, lying naked on the mattress together. Time seemed to pause if only for a moment where we were just taking each other in. I looked him up and down, tracing the ink in his skin with my finger tips. I could tell he was doing the same. Never had I been with someone as tattooed as me and it was almost like looking in a mirror. Benji's body told a story and I wanted to learn all of it.

"I really like to please, may I?" as he laid down comfortably between my thighs, grabbing at my legs to move them out of the way, going in with his tongue to make me more wet than i already was. "You're so wet" he said it like I didn't already know it, "I love the way you taste" he snuck in before going right back into indulging in my juices. Time was standing still again. Little jolts of electricity seemed to surge through my body as he kept licking and sucking my pussy. That feeling was completely coming over me, my heart rate felt higher, my breath changing, my clit throbbing. I came and he kept going. "I am just getting started with you" he said as he inserted two fingers while still eating me out like my pussy was his first meal after a week long fast. Screaming now with my eyes rolling back as this man just keeps giving me more and more pleasure.

A typical hookup usually goes something like, the guy comes over, jack hammer rails the girl, gets his nut and leaves, the girl left unsatisfied, so a man in my red room right now giving me repeated pleasure driven orgasms without taking anything for himself yet was incredible.

"I'm gonna get it," Benji said as shoved his fingers in me deeper and faster, in and out repeatedly, determination in his face looking between me with my eyes rolling back and his fingers playing a disappearing act inside of me. "Almost there, almost got it," my moans grew louder and louder until suddenly a waterfall of fluid came gushing out of me all over his hand, "There we go, that's a good girl" Benji said gleaming with pride. Clearly he was into squirt, and it seemed he had the magic touch to get it out of me.

Here I was, lying here absolutely spent, in my own little

RED FLAGS & ROSES

puddle, already used to filth before he had even used me in any way for his own pleasure. So many thoughts running through my head. How did we even get here? This was not how I anticipated my night going when Alejandra suggested we go out. I was going to have to catch Jake up on so much tomorrow. I was going to have to catch Alejandra up as well whenever I was to make it back to my own bed. Wishfully I was hoping that this would happen again, and soon, and we weren't even done with this moment right now. Pleasure Dom's were hard to come by and Benji being one was unexpected but I already knew I would have to hold onto this one for dear life.

Lost in my own thoughts I almost forgot Benji was still here, now climbing on top of me inserting himself inside of me. "You got a little bit left for me?" he asked with a sly tone suggesting I looked tired and done. I was tired, and generally done, but lost in subspace. I would let this man do anything he wanted to me. "Use me" came from my lips in a whisper as he thrusted his pulsing cock inside of me. "Use me please, fucking use me!" I blurted out louder than before. I felt him twitch inside of me, he wrapped his hands around my throat, made direct eye contact with me, and said "You are my pet, I will use you however I'd like." All the while he kept railing me until moaning, "Fuck, I'm so close," under his breath, now thrusting faster and harder into me. "Please Benji, fill me" I begged with consent, hoping he would finish inside of me. I'm such a little cum slut and I just wanted to lay in the filth we created together with our bodies. He moaned out louder now with a final pushing thrust, I could feel his cock quivering inside of me as he filled me. "That's a good girl. Take all of me." he said, still locking eyes with mine.

He finished and rolled to the side of me. Our bodies next to each other, still touching slightly with warm skin to skin contact. I leaned my head on his chest, he ran his fingers through my hair. I had no idea what time it was, but exhausted from sex, drinking, lack of sleep, I felt myself dozing off in his arms.

After some time, likely not long, I began to stir more awake coming out of subspace. The morning light tiptoed through the curtains, painting delicate patterns on the walls from the stained glass window cling. The air was still heavy with the residue of the night, it smelled like sweat and sex. Beside me, Benji, his voice, raw and vulnerable, cut through the quiet. "Callie, last night, er, this morning, was... something else."

I turned toward him, the sheets a tangled mess around us. "Yeah, it really was."

There was a hesitation in his gaze, a weight that settled between us. "I just want to make sure we're on the same page here," he began, his words measured but full of uncertainty. "I'm not really in a place for another relationship right now, especially after Em and I..."

His voice trailed off. I reached out, my fingers tracing invisible lines on his arm, offering a silent reassurance. "I get it, Benji. I'm not looking for anything serious either," I replied, my tone soft yet resolute. "We both know what this is."

That was the truth, my life was very fulfilling with Jake and Alejandra, and i dint have a lot of free time for a third partner. But Benji was something special, different, unique. If he was interested in more, I already knew I could make the time to make this work. I already craved more of what happened last night.

He nodded, a mix of relief and gratitude flashing in his eyes. "I just needed to be clear about it."

The space between us felt different now—despite the inti-

19

macy we had shared, a new layer of boundaries had been drawn, delineating the path of what this connection could be. I had to play it cool.

At this point it had been over 24 hours of me being awake, I found myself dozing off to sleep again now nuzzled under Benji's arm. I comfortably drifted off to sleep feeling safe in his arms.

I woke up a few hours later to Benji at the edge of the bed putting his socks and shoes on. "Hey I have to head out, I ordered an Uber I didn't wanna wake you, sorry." There was a sadness to his voice, I couldn't quite put my finger on it. Maybe I was overthinking things already wanting more than I agreed to be okay with.

Benji headed for the door, but leaned into me in bed and gave me a quick kiss. "Truly, I needed this. I had a great time. We should do this again soon." As Benji left, I felt a little bittersweet. Alone in the wake of our encounter, I found solace in the quiet reflection of the evening— I started to tidy up the red room, stripped the bed and brought the linens upstairs to wash. I started a load of laundry, soiled sex stained sheets, before climbing back into my actual bed upstairs with Alejandra still soundly asleep. I laid down next to her determined to get some more sleep, excited to wake up and share with her all the festivities of the night.

Chapter 2: 8/13

Part One

The afternoon light spilled lazily through the half-closed blinds, painting stripes across the crumpled sheets where I lay. My head throbbed with the residue of a night that had been as intoxicating as the alcohol I had shared with friends at The Social and then some more back at the house.

Alejandra's side of the bed was empty. It was 3 o'clock in the afternoon after all, but staying up until the crack of dawn with Benji was absolutely worth the messed up sleep schedule.

Sitting up, I reached for my phone, the screen revealing several missed messages in the throuple group chat from both Jake and Alejandra alike.

"She took Benji home last night! Yes that Benji!"

"Omg I can't wait until she's awake to fill us in I have to know the details"

"I wonder what time they went to bed last night, we got home around two in the morning I think so I bet they had a late night."

I stared at their messages, stirring awake a little more now, trying to figure out a witty response to the gossip of my partners already knowing the basics of my sexual escapades last night.

"LOL good morning guys, yes, me and Benji had sex last night, idk what is gonna come of this, seems like just casual fun for right now. I'll fill you both in on the details later not over text. Love you both." I hit send and put my phone aside, I heard Alejandra rummaging in the other room, likely cleaning or working on one of her puzzles. Today was definitely going to be a day to relax. I needed to eat something, see what Alejandra was getting into, and catch her up on everything. I could tell Jake the details later either on Face Time or in another two days when he was set to return home from his work trip.

A ping interrupted my thoughts—a message from Benji. My heart quickened as I unlocked my phone, hoping for something more than a casual remark or a witty joke. But as I read the message, I exhaled in disappointment. It was a cheeky comment about last night's antics, nothing more. "Thanks for letting me cum over last night haha, let's do it again sometime soon." He didn't give much away, perpetuating the playful distance he suggested we maintain.

Pushing the sheets aside, I swung my legs over the edge of the bed, feeling a mix of reluctance and anticipation about the day ahead. Benji's allure was undeniable, his charm infectious, but I was not excited to get roasted by my partners for having new relationship energy about an emotionally unavailable man. Especially when this was not a relationship. But I know they'll see right through me. With a sigh, I got out of bed and readied myself for the day, slipping into a cozy pair of sweatpants and an over sized shirt.

I headed towards the kitchen to get some coffee, I heard Alejandra downstairs, took my pills, and headed down to join her to face the inevitable conversation. As suspected she was working on a puzzle. Her focus always astounded me, a beautiful blend of precision and patience.

"Morning," I said softly, trying to gauge her mood.

Alejandra glanced up, a smile gracing her lips. "Hey, sleepy-head. It's the afternoon. Long night?"

"Actually, yeah, it was."

Setting the tray table with the puzzle on it aside, she motioned for me to join her. "I saw your little text in the group chat. Tell me everything. I've been dying to hear about your evening. What time did you make it to bed?"

I settled into the couch right next to her, fiddling with the handle of my coffee mug. "It was... unexpected. Benji and I, we got talking, and then one thing led to another..."

Alejandra's gaze softened, her eyes encouraging me to continue. "And?"

"We ended up in the red room," I confessed, watching her reaction closely.

She nodded, her expression unchanged. "And?"

"We slept together," I blurted out, surprised by the tension in my voice. "It just happened. I didn't plan for it to, but it did."

Alejandra reached out, covering my hand with hers. "Callie, it's okay. I trust you. I just hope that you had a good time."

Relief washed over me, mingling with gratitude for her understanding. "Thank you for being so amazing about this. I was worried about how you'd take it." I had not seen anyone new since I started dating Alejandra, so despite our non monogamous relationship boundaries, I was still worried about her reaction.

She offered a reassuring smile. "We've talked about this, remember? Openness, honesty—it's what we value. I've just been here working on my puzzle while you were sleeping just awaiting you to tell me all of the details."

Her words eased the weight off my chest. "I love you, Alejandra."

"I love you too," she replied, squeezing my hand gently.

As we sat there in the quiet comfort of our shared space, I realized how fortunate I was to have Alejandra by my side, accepting and supportive. Our polyamorous journey was unconventional to many, but to us, it was a canvas we painted with trust, understanding, and love.

"So, are you gonna tell me about Benji," Alejandra prompted gently, her eyes fixed on mine.

I took a deep breath, the words stumbling out as I attempted to piece together the complexities of my feelings. "It was fun, relaxed, like... comfortable, you know? We laughed, shared stories, it felt... natural, effortless. But the sex was something else, it was something out of a movie. It was like a dance we had choreographed and perfected over weeks and months of practice. I've never had sex like that in my life before, and I am certain it wasn't because of the liquor." I continued to tell her all the details, not holding back at all.

Alejandra's expression, seemingly a mix of understanding and curiosity. She was always great at feeling compersion instead of jealousy. "And where does Benji stand in all of this?"

"He made it clear, Alejandra." I swallowed hard, the truth almost bitter on my tongue. "He doesn't want anything serious, just something casual."

Her gaze lingered on me, a silent understanding passing between us. "And what about you, Callie?"

The question hung in the air, I hadn't fully unraveled myself. "I... I don't know," I admitted, my voice barely above a whisper.

"I mean, it's fine. I'm okay with being casual, right?"

Alejandra reached out, her hand finding mine, grounding me in her support. "Are you sure about that? You seem like there might be more brewing beneath the surface."

I sighed, feeling the weight of my already conflicting emotions. "Maybe... maybe I do want more, Alejandra. But I can't expect that from Benji. He was very clear about what he wanted last night, but he has said he wants to see me again."

Her thumb traced soothing circles on the back of my hand. "It's okay to want more, Callie. Your feelings are valid. But you have to respect what he wants too and I just don't wanna see you getting hurt in all of this."

A sense of relief washed over me, mingled with a surge of vulnerability at admitting my desires. "I'm scared of complicating things. Between us, between everything."

"We thrive in complexity, remember?" Alejandra's voice held a reassuring certainty. "We've navigated intricate emotions before. This is just another layer."

"I don't want to disappoint you or Jake," I confessed, my voice tinged with worry. Benji came through with a one night stand and he already felt like he was going to be a major wrench in all the gears.

Alejandra shook her head gently. "Callie, you could never disappoint us by being honest about your feelings. That's what we value most—openness, authenticity."

I nodded, continuously grateful for her understanding, yet still grappling with the turmoil within. "What do I do now?"

"We'll figure it out together," Alejandra replied, her voice a comforting melody amidst the chaos of my thoughts. "See if he'll wanna come over again tonight, if he comes back over in less than 24 hours maybe he wants more than he says he does.

25

Maybe he feels similar to how you feel but he just needs a little more time."

The notion felt daunting, but the idea of clarity appealed to me. "I'll text him and ask," I affirmed, a newfound determination flickering within.

Alejandra smiled, a softness in her eyes that spoke volumes. "Whatever happens, me and Jake are here for you. Always."

As I sipped my coffee, and Alejandra resumed her puzzle, my fingers hovered over my phone, a silent battle raging within me. I again found myself staring at the screen, the innocuous text from Benji earlier burning into my thoughts. "Thanks for letting me cum over last night haha, let's do it again sometime soon?" The casual tone, the nonchalant suggestion of hooking up again, was inviting him over the next night too much?

I typed, deleted, and retyped my response multiple times, each attempt being an intricate battle between nonchalance and raw honesty. Finally, with a shaky exhale, I hit send, a simple yet calculated message: "I had a good time too. If you're free tonight, I don't have any plans yet. I know you said we should do things again, not sure if a day later is too soon."

My heart hammered in my chest, anxiety bubbling as I awaited his reply. Seconds stretched into eternity. I scolded myself for caring so much, for craving his presence when I knew it was only supposed to be temporary and casual.

A ping of my phone broke the silence, and I felt my pulse quickening as I read his response.

"Hey yea that sounds nice, I can come over around 9!"

The anticipation coiled around me like a tightening knot, the seconds ticking by at an agonizingly slow pace. Benji's affirmation of my invitation to come over again tonight reverberated in my mind. Alejandra was lounging on the couch, taking a break from her puzzle again, her eyes fixed on me, "So, you're blushing, he's coming over again?"

I nodded, a flutter of nervousness in my chest. "Yeah, around 9. He said he'll be here."

Her lips curved into a mischievous smile. "Mind if I join in for a bit? I could use a drink and some company."

Alejandra and Benji—, intersecting in a moment of uncertainty. "Are you sure? I mean, it might be... weird."

She shrugged, the nonchalant gesture belying the curiosity in her eyes. "Not weird unless you want it to be. Besides, we hit it off last night when I shared a drink with you too. What's the harm in hanging out again? I'll leave you to be when things start to heat up."

"Okay, sure. It'll be nice."

Part Two

As the clock ticked closer to 9, I fidgeted with the couch cushions, my nerves on edge. Alejandra poured herself a glass of wine, clearly not at all nervous unlike myself. The soft knock on the door startled me, and my heart skipped a beat as I glanced at Alejandra, a silent exchange of anticipation passing between us. I hurried to the door, my hand trembling slightly as I turned the knob, revealing Benji's silhouette against the faint glow of the foyer.

"Hey," he greeted with that familiar smirk that sent a jolt of electricity through me.

"Hi," I replied, trying to keep my voice steady, my eyes flickering back to Alejandra, who offered a friendly wave from the couch.

"Come on in, welcome back" I said, stepping aside to let him enter.

Benji's eyes darted briefly toward Alejandra before settling back on me.

"Hope you don't mind, Alejandra wanted to hang out with us for a bit tonight. Jake, who I was telling you about last night, is still out of town so I told her if she was lonely she could crash our little party." a white lie but I wanted to sound cool and calculated.

Glasses clinked as we sipped, Alejandra still working on a bottle of wine, me and Benji enjoying some whiskey mainly as a hair of the dog from the shot's we did the night before. I found myself entangled in a web of conflicting emotions—gratitude for Alejandra's presence, yet a yearning for something more with Benji. I caught glances between Alejandra and Benji as well, which was fine, a twinge of jealousy sure, but all in good graces. Me and Alejandra shared Jake as a partner after all and we were drinking quite a bit. I think she just missed the presence of a man around. Maybe my anxiety was getting the better of me and it was nothing.

The hours slipped by, conversations meandered through various topics, and the initial awkwardness dissolved into a comfortable familiarity.

"Thanks for hanging out with us," I murmured in Benji's direction.

"It's been nice getting to know you and one of your partners more, it's a shame Jake couldn't join us," he replied, his voice holding a hint of something secret. His interest in even hanging out with Jake caught me off guard. Usually men specifically feel a bit weird about fucking me and me having a husband. Those uneducated about non-monogamy think that my husband is going to be mad because they assume I am cheating before wrapping their minds around polyamorous relationships.

"Well we can always do this again next weekend, maybe you can invite your best friend Chad over and we can all play darts in the garage or something. If we're gonna keep hooking up I'm sure Jake will enjoy meeting you." Suggesting we'd keep hooking up was a bit of a hopeful reach, but man was I hopeful.

"Well, speaking of, I don't know all the rules of this lifestyle yet so I mean no harm when I suggest this, but are we going to hook up tonight...?" his glance then moving from me to Alejandra, "And is this going to be a party of three? Au ménage à trois?"

"Uh, Benji..." I stammered, my mind racing to find the right words, but somehow not opposed to the idea completely.

Alejandra's gaze flickered between me and him, her jaw tight. "Seriously?"

I shifted on the couch feeling the weight of the situation bearing down on me. "I... I didn't expect... this," I murmured.

Benji leaned back, trying to diffuse the awkwardness. "I just thought... with the chemistry and all, it could be fun."

As Benji's voice trailed off, the room fell into an abrupt silence, each word echoing louder in my mind. Alejandra's widened eyes mirrored my own astonishment.

Benji shifted in his seat, his eyes darting between us, gauging our reactions. "I'm sorry, maybe it seems like I'm stepping on Jake's toes while he's not here, I swear that's not what I'm trying to do, I don't know what I'm doing, we've had some drinks and I thought the energy was there with Alejandra joining us all night and I've never had a threesome before and now I'm just rambling awkwardly, maybe I should leave."

29

"I... I think we should talk, me and Callie real fast, don't leave yet Benji just give us a minute," Alejandra finally said, her voice tentative yet resolute.

Benji nodded understandingly, excusing himself momentarily to give us space. "I gotta use the restroom anyways, I'll give you two a moment."

"I don't know what to think," Alejandra admitted to me, her eyes searching for reassurance in mine. "I'm not opposed to exploring this with you, Callie. But only if you feel the same way."

"I'm... I'm not sure either," I confessed, the admission hanging between us, we both broke the uncertainty with a bomb of laughter. "Fuck it right, we should do this? It's Benji, he's hot, he was GREAT last night, it's just casual." I suggested.

"Yea, let's give this man his first threesome." Alejandra said more enthusiastically now.

Benji returned, his eyes reflected a mix of anticipation and respect for our deliberation.

"You wanna give us another moment and meet us in the red room?" I said to him with promise in my tone of us both joining him.

"Okay," he said, a hint of excitement tingling in his voice.

He walked nervously to the red room, looking back at us both catching glances of us smirking at him.

"We'll be there in a minute" I said looking over the edge of my glass taking the final sips from my whiskey. Alejandra and I were giggling. This was a normal drill for us, after all, we were in a throuple with a man and threesomes were kinda the norm for us. It was entertaining that the one weekend Jake is gone on a trip we manage to get ourselves into a little bit of trouble with a new man to share.

30

"We're about to change Benji's life, Callie, you know that right?"

"Oh I am so ready." thinking if anything this would just be some harmless kinky fun, but maybe, just maybe, this could amount to so much more.

Alejandra stood up from the couch, placing her now empty glass down on a coaster on the coffee table. "Alright let's do this" she said, extending her hand out to mine to help me up off the couch.

My hand in hers, I followed her down the dark hall into the red room. Benji was sitting at the edge of the bed waiting on us, shirtless. His silver jeweled chain adorned around his neck sparkled in the red lights. He had put his long hair up into a bun and his jeans were unbuttoned but still sat high on his hips. It was clear he was conflicted about taking them off so preemptively. I would have expected him to be a little more nervous on the surface considering this was his first threesome but he still held himself together.

Alejandra and I both sat down on either side of him, as queer women we didn't like adding to the rhetoric of male dominated threesomes and us just existing for the male gaze but at this moment it seemed that we telepathically understood the assignment of just spoiling this man for whatever reason. It was fun sometimes especially when it was on our terms and we were in cahoots together about it.

I leaned across Benji to grab Alejandra and kiss her, soft at first, lips locked in passion. Maybe we were putting a bit of a show on for Benji. He leaned back a little, noticeably enjoying what he was watching but also just giving us our space. Alejandra pulled away from kissing me and in a smooth pull over her neck and head tore her shirt right off. Her breasts

31

were supple and hung delicately. She was nowhere near as tattooed as me or Benji, but had just a few herself. Taking off her shirt revealed a large floral chest piece previously unknown to Benji. His eyes lit up at her naked in front of him, probably a combination of him admiring the art that was inked across her chest, or you know, maybe it was just the fact that her chest was out there for him to see and feel.

I followed her decision to take off her own top and took off my own. We sat there as a trio, all shirtless and bare just admiring each other. All of us being intricately adorned with our own tattoos not apparent to the average person. Tattoos noticeable only to those that see you naked always hold such a weight of intimacy. Benji traced his fingers on Alejandra's chest just as I had done on his the evening before. I touched my hand to his jawline, turning his head to my direction, meeting my lips with his. He placed both of his hands around my face, kissing me back now with more passion than before. Distracted by my touch and my kiss, Alejandra took it upon herself to take off her own jeans and underwear while watching me and Benji make out. Out of the corner of my eye catching glances while I could, I saw her get on her knees in front of Benji, hands intently on his zipper, tugging at his pants to remove them. "Come on, you're way overdressed." She said as she tugged at them more, pulling them off over his ankles.

"Well now, Callie is the one that's over dressed" Benji proclaimed as I sat there still in my black cotton mini skirt and underwear. Still on her knees, Alejandra twisted her body to meet my waist and began tugging at my skirt, "Benji, grab the other side of it," the two of them taking off my last remaining articles of clothing together.

The three of us now naked among the glow of dim red lights,

I went right back to kissing Benji. I couldn't get enough of the way he tasted as he kissed me back while biting at my bottom lip.

Alejandra loved sucking dick, I didn't hate it but let's just say she was better than me, and unlike me, actually enjoyed giving it. I was no throat goat like she was. I pulled back from kissing Benji to lean my head on his shoulder for a minute. Watching Alejandra suck dick was an art form and I wanted to see her perform and watch as she'd pull Benji into a pleasure trance.

She began slow, but precise, taking all of him in her mouth. "F-Fuck, pleas-" Benji could hardly make words. She kept sucking him, her wide brown eyes looking up at him and glancing at me still snuggled up on his shoulder. He was too in touch with what was happening to make eye contact back to her and it's almost like that's what she was hoping for. She took all of him now, a near seven girthy inches down the back of her throat, not a single flinch or gag. Benji's eyes rolled in the back of his head and he groaned loudly. It seemed that he realized he could use her face as he pleased. He grabbed a fistful of her dark brown hair and began pounding the back of her throat. A face full of cock and she was smiling ear to ear.

Alejandra pulled herself away from Benji's dick and wiped the spit off her lips. She proceeded to get up, climb into bed, and position herself onto her back and opened her legs wide. "Well, who's gonna give me head now?"

I was in there as quick as could be, on all fours face deep in her pussy which was absolutely sopping wet. While bent over in between Alejandra's thighs, Benji decided to get up and position himself behind me. He starts to rub my clit almost as if to see if I am wet already, which I practically was the second he walked in my house. He touches me gently but in all the right places slightly distracting me from eating my girlfriend's pretty pussy. I put my hands around Alejandra's waist as I pull her closer to me as she quivers, I felt her shaking and she started cumming from what I was doing.

I waited until she was screaming before I myself took a step back, but instead of wiping my face off I turned to Benji and said "want to taste her?" right before shoving my tongue down his throat.

Benji kissed me back for a second before shoving his hands at my chest, pushing me back on the bed on my back. "Your turn" he said. He proceeds to get into the same position that I was just in for Alejandra, he's on all fours, slips two fingers inside of me, and begins to work on my clit with his tongue. His fingers feel like magic, the combination of his fingers and tongue are insanity.

Just as I start to cum, I grind into Benji's face harder I start moaning his name, begging for his cock, begging him to fuck me.

"Well, well, well, you're very eager for that cock huh Callie?" Mocked Alejandra at me. I knew she was going to make fun of my eagerness for a while.

"You don't understand, you NEED to try his face out, the fingers he has, I just— wow, it's like he learned from a lesbian how to finger and eat pussy."

"Well let's put him to the test then or see if it's just you that feels this way, my turn again." Alejandra said as she grabbed Benji by his bun and shoved his face in between her legs. He didn't seem to mind.

I decided my second orgasm was merely moments away, so while my girlfriend was on her back receiving head from Benji, I took it upon myself to take a seat on her face and ride her lips with mine. As I grinded her face, she moaned into my crotch. She wasn't great at multitasking and it was obvious Benji was distracting her but her soft tongue on my clit still felt so good. I kept riding her face determined to see the end of my second orgasm.

I ever so gracefully dismounted from my position to give her as breather. I was too distracted by my own pleasure to notice the intricacies of her cumming underneath me from Benji but based on her breathing patterns it happened.

"Wow, I— I really want more of that tongue, lay down, let me ride your face while Callie rides your cock."

He didn't mind not having a say in what was happening, in fact I think he enjoyed being bossed around a little bit because he listened to the orders with zero hesitation.

Benji now laying down on his back, Alejandra now riding his face, while facing me, I climbed on top to ride his cock like my life depended on it. I slid his member into my tight wet pussy, and I began to ride him in cowgirl position. I was facing Alejandra and we could catch glimpses of each other in pleasure while both riding different ends of this man together.

Underneath us both, Benji reached up and was able to grab Alejandra's tits and squeeze them which sent her into letting out an incredibly loud moan. She came again, not uncommon for her to have multiple orgasms back to back, and rolled over off his face to lay down and take another breather.

Benji now just had me to focus on, moving his hands toward my clit, rubbing left to right again and again as I continued to bounce on top of him. Fuck it felt good. "Oh fuck yes! Just like that! Keep going! Faster!!" I was so close, I was right there, and then he pulled his hands to my sides, picked me up off of him, flipped me over on my back, and began to slide his cock back inside of me and rail me harder and harder. Alejandra picked up on the situation at hand and became Benji's assistant in helping make me cum again. He was railing into me as Alejandra teased and flicked my clit with her left hand and placed her mouth around one of my nipples. She was biting and flicking with her tongue. Nipple stimulation brought me to orgasm so quickly and I found myself squirting all over Benji's cock. "Woah!! You really are a squirter!" He cooed.

He looked at Alejandra and said "let's see if you are too" as he pushed her down and dragged her closer to him. He slide himself inside of her and began to fuck her harder and faster than he had just fucked me, it was clear he was close to blowing his load and that became the mission. I placed my right hand around my girlfriend's throat, just enough pressure to both shut her up and keep her still. She struggled to moan through my choking but still let out whimpers as he fucked her. Benji's breath changed, "fuck I'm so close" as he kept at it with Alejandra.

"You're doing such a good job for him, being his little toy, his pet." I learned the night before that he liked that kind of ownership talk in an objectification kink kind of way. And sure thing, just as I said it, he pulled out and blew his load of cum all over Alejandra's lower stomach.

"You were such a good girl for him." I praised her right before I bent over to lick the cum from her torso. I am such a little cum slut and I wasn't about to let an ounce of it go to waste. I started with a preliminary lick as if to taste test it and then I really went for it.

When I was done licking all of Benji's juices off of Alejandra, I joined them both in laying down in bed. We all audibly let out a giggle simultaneously almost as if we just had processed what had happened.

"Callie you said he was good this morning, but, wow, yea—you were right! Good job Benji!"

"Yea, Benji, I wanna keep doing this with you..."

"That's totally fine with me. I want to keep doing this with you too, but damn, you two wore me out I am exhausted. Mind if I just crash here?"

Alejandra and I agreed he could stay, after all that's what the red room was for. I really wanted to snuggle him and stay with him but he was dozing off quickly and the bed had a dozen wet spots. I gave him a generally friendly kiss goodnight, grabbed a dry blanket for him, a glass of water, and bid him adieu for the rest of the evening knowing he would likely be gone by time I woke up.

Me and Alejandra walked up stairs naked, our clothes in our hands, ready for our last night together in bed just the two of us before Jake was to come home the next day. We had a lot to catch him up on, way more than we had anticipated.

"Tonight was a lot of fun, I can see why you're into him. I hope you still feel good about me joining."

"Yea that was a good time, it was interesting to have a threesome with you and a different man than Jake, I had a good time!"

"We're going to have to update him on a whole lot tomorrow when his flight lands and he gets home."

"Yea let's give him a minute to settle in and we'll catch him up."

We drifted off to sleep, well, Alejandra noticeably by her soft snores did at least. I was left awake staring at the ceiling in the dark, listening to the soft hum of the fan, seeing the shadows of the tree outside of my window dance delicately across my walls in the moonlight. It felt good to sleep next to Alejandra, but something inside of me felt pulled in two directions, like maybe I was supposed to stay downstairs with Benji.

My head was racing full of thoughts. We didn't do anything wrong per the boundaries of our polyamorous relationship, but I was so nervous to see Jake tomorrow and tell him everything for some odd reason. Benji on paper was everything I ever wanted, the closest person to perfection in my eyes that I had ever engaged with and I knew being honest about that was going to drive Jake into a little bit of jealousy, rightfully so. Oh well, a problem for tomorrow, and at least Alejandra would be with me to help.

Chapter 3: 8/25

Jake was now home, a little more than a week had passed since my first hookup with Benji and then the threesome with him and Alejandra the next night. Jake had been home for a handful of days now, and we were very excited to have him back and had spent the week updating him on all the little things that happened while he was gone. He was fully up to date on the happenings of Benji mingling in our lives, and I could tell there was a twinge of jealousy as I anticipated, but he handled it fairly well. I can't blame him for the bit of lingering jealousy, I mean he left for a few days and this new suave man came in suddenly and unexpectedly, and then fucked his wife and girlfriend.

We were hosting a little game night tonight though and it was my super smart idea to have invited Benji to bridge the differences. After all, Benji was someone I wanted to keep around even if only for my own selfish sexual desires and I wanted him and Jake to be familiar with each other at the minimum. I had only gushed about him all week to my husband, myself caught in lust, and I just needed them to meet each other.

The evening air hummed with anticipation as I prepared for game night. "Benji's on his way he says he's about 15 minutes out, and he's bringing his friend Chad. It's going to be fun!" I said after looking up from the text on my phone and then putting it back in my pocket.

Jake raised an eyebrow, intrigued. "Chad? I don't think I've met him before or even heard of him."

"He's a riot," Alejandra chimed in. "You'll like him. I met him briefly that night when me and Callie went to The Social. He's Benji's best friend and roommate!"

"Oh yes that's right, you girls did briefly tell me about him."

Then the doorbell chimed, signaling Benji's arrival. I jumped up, excitement bubbling within me. "That must be them!"

I opened the door, greeted Benji with a warm hug, followed by introductions between him and Jake, and then Chad and Jake. As they arrived, the air seemed to thicken. Poor Chad was just along for the ride but it was probably good to have an extra person in the mix unaffiliated to what was going on. We needed someone to neutralize any tension. I welcomed them with a carefully curated smile, though my insides twisted in knots. Benji's eyes flickered between Jake and Alejandra, a subtle unease cloaked beneath his charming facade.

Throughout the evening, among the card games we were playing as a group of five, I found myself snuggling up closer to Benji on the couch, Chad mainly oblivious to the intricacies of what was happening, and Alejandra keeping Jake occupied. Chad proved to be an entertaining addition to the group, effortlessly blending in with his easy going nature. Benji seemed more relaxed than usual, probably because his best friend was with him, and Jake kept making eyes at the subtle glances exchanged between Benji and I.

"Let's do a round of shots and play some darts!" I suggested wanting to liven things up and get us all up off the couch.

Nobody was opposed to my suggestion, and everyone hopped right up. "Now we're talking," said Benji.

"What do you like to drink?" Jake asked Benji, probably the first direct thing they said to each other all night. My two men talking to each other sent flutters directly to my clit.

"Oh a little bit of everything but mainly whiskey, I'm a big fan of Crown Royal."

Thank god. They had something in common.

"Oh shit me too! Let's do a shot of that together!" Jake seemed impressed that he had good taste both in whiskey and women. I was just happy to see them communicating and not at each other's throats. I had dated other men before, and Jake, a queer man himself, definitely had no problem with more men in the polycule but something about Benji was just different and I didn't want any tension between them.

Seeing them interact and getting along had my imagination running wild though, I found myself daydreaming of the two of them spit roasting me, taking turns using me. I could just imagine how good Benji would feel, pulsing inside of my pussy while Jake's familiar cock penetrated my ass. Maybe Alejandra would join in and sit on my face while the men stretched out my holes. I visibly had to shake my whole head to calm the intrusive horny thoughts down and remember that I was just enjoying a casual game night right now and not a mini orgy.

"You okay Callie?" asked Benji, concerned as we stepped into the garage.

"Oh yea just a weird thought, I'm okay, throwing some darts will help."

We played for a while, enjoying pretty basic conversation before Jake, my sleepy old man, decided to turn in for bed. "Hey man, it was great to meet you" shaking Benji's hand, "and you too!" gesturing a wave at Chad, "but it's eleven o'clock and I am truly shocked at myself that I even made it this long, I'm gonna head to bed."

"If you'll excuse me for a minute, I'll be right back down!" I said as I followed Jake back inside the house from the garage and up the stairs to bed to say goodnight to him in private, but also I inquired how he felt about Benji. "He seems really nice! I like him based on what I know so far, go enjoy your evening with him, don't worry about me, I'm just tired!"

I came back downstairs to the living room and the energy felt shifted, Jake in bed, it was just four of us, Benji and I, as well as Chad and Alejandra and it definitely started to feel more like a double date.

"Hey, I think we're going to head out soon. It's getting late for us too," said Benji, struggling to make eye contact with me. The liquor had me desperately wanting him more than ever. My head was full of horny thoughts from imagining a foursome earlier with Benji and both of my partners. I brushed up to him and said "But I thought we'd hookup tonight, you don't wanna fuck me before you leave?" I was trying my best to coerce him into staying just a bit longer until my needs were met. I know he brought Chad with him, but I was under the impression that we were definitely fuck buddies, and if he left without sex this would be the first time we ever just hung out together without fucking.

"Do you want to make me squirt at least before you go?" His eyes widened when he watched me do that before as if it was sorcery, and I felt like that's how I could reel him in for some fun.

"You know, I guess that can be arranged." He said.

"Okay Daddy, follow me" I said as I started to skip towards the red room. Did I just call him Daddy? I'll unpack that later. He didn't seem to question it and was already following me.

"Do you want to watch the show?" I suggested it as an open gesture to Alejandra and Chad. I think Alejandra would've passed and let me and Benji enjoy some one on one time but Chad abruptly stood up, slammed his drink, and said "Do I ever, wow, your life is so interesting, is that a serious offer?"

"Yea I mean I don't mind and we're all hanging out and I don't want anyone to feel left out, did Benji tell you about the red room?"

I turned back towards the red room continuing my walk down the hall with Benji, Chad and Alejandra shortly behind us. I began to undress myself as a tease in front of Benji, brushing my hands down his chest, lightly taunting his crotch and grabbing. I turned around to take off my pants and placed my ass right on the growing bulge in his pants. I slowly pulled my pants down, bending further and further forward, rubbing my ass more and more on his crotch feeling him grow. I was determined to get more than just what he signed up for.

Naked now, I turned around, kissed him once, and laid myself down in bed. "Are you going to do that magical thing you do with your fingers and make your favorite toy put on a squirt show for these two?"

He crawled to me in the center of bed, lapping up the juices of my pussy like a kitten to its milk. He slipped 2 fingers deep inside of me, my back arching. My moans intensified as he made a "come here" motion with two digits inside of me, "You're doing so good already baby," he whispered in praise. "You're taking my fingers so well, you're fucking dripping for me, I know you're just dying for more…"

His words had my eyes rolling back and my toes curling. "Oh fuck, OH FUCK," I was so close, but it was taking a little bit of extra work, I don't normally do this with an audience after all

43

and my head was full of questions, like for starters, have Chad and Benji been sexual in the same room together before this moment?

Suddenly, two fingers on his right hand still inside of me, he reached up with his left, slapped me hard in the face before placing his hand around my throat. He growled, "C'mon, be a good girl and cum for me," and that was enough to send me over the edge. My pussy erupted like a volcano, soaking Benji, his hair sopping wet, as well as the sheets between him and I. That's what I needed. I can't believe he slapped me, more so, I can't believe I liked it that much.

"Fuck, that was so hot. Squirting is like my favorite kink." proclaimed Chad.

Alejandra, clearly very horny as well now, made the shocking suggestion, "Well, what do you say we keep this going? Chad, do you want to make this a friendly competition and see if you can help me squirt quicker and more?"

Chad looked like he saw a ghost for a quick moment while processing, but then reacted properly by picking Alejandra up, laying her down on the bed in a dry spot he could find, ripping her pants and panties off with a swiftness, and immediately shoving his fingers inside of her. He didn't hesitate. He didn't question it, he just ran with it. All while I just laid in Benji's arms coming to my senses after squirting so hard.

"Well, they are doing that, you made me feel good, let me help you feel good now?" I said, getting off the bed and on my knees. Benji got up and stood before me, "Really I should be headed out." His noticeably hard cock in his pants suggested otherwise. He had to wait for his friend and my girlfriend to be done with their little play session before he could leave anyways. I placed my hands on his thighs, worshiping him. He was Daddy. I could see that clearly now.

"Daddy," I said subtly and slowly, "please let me satisfy you, a mere thank you for always being so good to me." Looking up at him I could see him biting on his lower lip, eyes closed, I had him right where I wanted him. I took off his pants and boxers, revealing a fully erect cock, quivering. I grabbed it in my right hand and licked the underside of it with my tongue. His hands fell at his side, one reaching for my hair, pulling me to suck more of him. A loud groan of pleasure escaped him as I did my best to take all of him in my mouth. He started attempting to fuck my face, holding my jaw in his hands. I gagged, and placed my hand around the base of his cock, jerking off what I couldn't handle in my mouth. I continued stroking the base of his shaft while tantalizing the frenum and tip. I wasn't the throat goat Alejandra was, but I was determined to have him blow his load on my tongue. My lips wrapped around the tip, I bobbed and bobbed, his cock nestled in my mouth, almost touching my throat.

"Fuck that feels good, goddamn you're going to make me bust," words I took as encouragement to keep going, bobbing more and more, twisting my hand around the base simultaneously. His hands around my head, grabbing at my hair in sections like handlebars. "Callie, fuck, FUCK Callie, Fu—" he busted his load in my mouth, his warm cum sliding down my throat. He pulled out of my mouth and a little extra dripped out of the tip of his cock like an oozing trickle and I went right back to it, licking it off of him with a huge smile on my face and my eyeliner running down my cheeks. He slapped his now half-flaccid cock wetly against my lips. "You're incredible, you know that right?"

"It's my pleasure to take care of you Daddy."

"Oh my god, OH MY GOD, FUCK, please don't stop" begged Alejandra, me and Benji looked questionably over at her getting railed by Chad. Me and him were so in tune with each other I had completely forgotten that his best friend was here in the room with us fooling around with my girlfriend. Chad's cock was so deep inside of her, I couldn't even see what it really looked like, I just saw his curly pubes brushing against her shaved pussy. Her legs were up in the air on his shoulders.

"Please cum for me, please Chad please I'm begging for it." quite literally begged Alejandra as Benji and I watched, him holding me in his hands. Chad pulled out his throbbing cock with his right hand and proceeded to slap her pussy hard with it until a thick white cream oozed out of his cock coating her lower stomach.

"Fuck. That was good. Fuck! What the fuck just happened? Wow, Callie, thanks for letting me fuck your girlfriend, Alejandra fuck, thank you for letting me fuck you!" Chad was struggling to find words other than 'fuck' with his cum brain.

"We've been best friends for a dozen or so years and that's the first time I've ever seen your dick. Did we just have a foursome?" Benji questioned.

"I think so, also, I heard her call you Daddy, proud of you my sweet boy." Chad professed while pointing at me.

It was crazy how in tune I felt to Benji. I didn't even process anything else happening around me. I had blinders on, and ear plugs for that matter too. Truly I just blocked out everything and focused on him and his pleasure. We didn't even have full penetrative sex despite Chad AND Alejandra engaging in that right next to us. Here I was an hour earlier day dreaming of group sex, it at the precipice of my fingertips, and instead of indulging in my desires I just blocked everything else out except Benji.

Jake chose one hell of a time to head to bed, tomorrow was going to be another morning of updating him on a slutty night. I had never called a man Daddy before other than Jake, until tonight. I was falling in love with my fuck buddy so quickly and things were getting dangerous, but I couldn't get enough of Benji and I don't see myself slowing down anytime soon.

Chapter 4: 9/5

It was Tuesday, I didn't work tomorrow and I felt a strong urge to get into some trouble. It had been a little over a week since I had last seen Benji despite us occasionally texting each other or sending each other a meme. We hadn't really strongly talked about our incredible connection last encounter to where we didn't even notice two people fucking in the same room as us. It was just another thing brushed under the rug.

Alejandra and Jake were both planning on heading to bed early, as they weren't as fortunate to have the next day off, but I was determined to find some fun to get into unlike my partners. Should I go out? Hit up the local Tavern? Hit up a friend I haven't seen in a while, grab a late bite? Maybe Benji would be interested in coming over. Immediately all other plan ideas in comparison to texting Benji to see if he was free seemed insignificant.

My phone felt heavy in my hand typing out a well thought out casual text to him, cautious to not be too much, I couldn't handle rejection but was very well understanding that he might just be busy already. I was a little annoyed that over a week of texting daily he wasn't suggesting making time to hang out or hook up again, but oh well.

"Hey Benji! Don't know if you're doing anything tonight

but I'm planning on staying in and drinking, would love some company if you're free." Sent. My heart raced, staring at my phone anticipating my device to show me when his message was read. Seconds felt like hours, it was like watching a pot of water boil. Finally, "Read 5:05 PM" directly under my message. Then, the bubble of him texting back appeared. I was eagerly anticipating an enthusiastic yes.

"Sure Callie! I can head to your place around 7, one more time, what was your address again?" I was giddy. Immediately overthinking everything. Fuck, I needed to shower, I needed to shave, the living room could use some tidying, I needed to make ice. Jake and Alejandra were already giggling at my attitude and anxiety of hosting Benji this evening. "Usually new relationship energy is annoying but it's cute when you have it, it's a little funny too" Jake said mockingly but lovingly. "So your boyfriend not boyfriend is gonna be a recurring thing huh?" questioned Alejandra also in a jokingly mocking way.

"He's not my boyfriend! We're just friends."

"Yea okay, but you definitely wish he were." sighed Alejandra.

As 7 o'clock approached, I found myself not able to sit still. Should I text him and ask if he's on his way? Should I put on something nicer than my gray sweatpants and a cropped band t-shirt? I caught myself staring out the window next to the front door, eager to open it as soon as he pulled up. Pacing between the window and the couch, my phone pinged, "Hey sorry! Running late, be there soon."

I ran upstairs, kissed Alejandra and Jake goodnight, them both still mocking me in unison. A definite downside to polyamory is being clowned by your partners together when you are displaying "simp" behavior. I brushed my teeth and sprayed a nice vanilla scented body spray over my comfortable clothes hoping I wasn't overdoing it. Before I knew it, he was here. "Hey, just parked, I'm outside."

The night wrapped around us like a comforting shroud as Benji sauntered into my living room, his easy charm and sly grin signaling the start of another casual evening. It had been WEEKS since I felt him inside of me last, we didn't even have penetrative sex the last time we saw each other. I longed for the warmth of his hand around my neck again and was thrilled he was able to come over tonight.

Glasses clinked as we poured ourselves whiskey drinks, the amber liquid casting a warm glow in the dimly lit room. "Cheers to another night of profound conversations and witty banter," Benji quipped, raising his glass in a mock toast. The jokes of sophistication were extra comical when we both knew after two drinks we'd be covered in sweat in a sex stench filled room together. I chuckled at his impression of being a gentleman, settling into the familiar routine of playful exchanges and effortless camaraderie. The couch cushions were slipping apart underneath us and I found myself inching towards being closer to him slowly. Our conversations flowed seamlessly, each moment hitting with waves of strong emotions for me.

As the night wore on, Benji's guarded demeanor softened ever so slightly, unveiling slivers of vulnerability beneath his facade. He spoke of his childhood, the dreams he once harbored, and the complexities that sculpted his present. Maybe it was the liquor. Regardless of what it was, it was beautiful to see a man with so many walls break them down even if just a little bit right in front of me.

"I never thought I'd end up here, doing what I do," he confessed, his voice tinged with a hint of wistfulness. He didn't see anything good in himself. He didn't think he was a good artist, which is crazy to me because he's always booked out and always traveling to so many different conventions. How could he not think he's good?

"I also didn't anticipate ending up here in this city, my parents moved me out here when I was younger. Now I'm just kinda, well, here?"

Watching him break down some of his walls for me, maybe the act of being a person of substance wasn't an impression after all. Maybe this was him giving me a piece of value proving him to want more than just casual? I listened intently to his stories, cherishing these rare glimpses into the labyrinth of his mind, a world he seldom revealed. His vulnerability resonated with the hidden depths of my own emotions, tucked away to preserve the fragile balance we maintained. He was so mysterious to me and to hear any bit or piece of what made him who he is today had me falling to my knees for him, deeper and stronger than before.

Minutes melted into hours. We found ourselves at the precipice of a moment, teetering on the edge between ending the evening and parting ways, or would one of us make a move on the other to take things into the red room? The night wasn't explicitly sexual feeling, but he was here, and I wanted more of him.

He was laid across the couch, his legs in my lap so relaxed, scrolling through the archive of his Instagram showing me old photos and connecting the dots of his stories with imagery to pair.

"Do you think we should just call it a night?" I suggested tentatively, sensing the weight of me getting an orgasm or not hovering between us. I definitely invited him over for sex but

51

RED FLAGS & ROSES

the evening took a weird turn. I didn't mind but I was getting a little anxious.

Benji's gaze lingered on mine, his eyes searching for something. "Yeah, maybe it's better," he murmured, his voice laced with a hint of hesitation, him pulling his legs back off of me and sitting up slightly. The atmosphere crackled, a tricky balance between restraint and longing. We hovered in that ambiguous space, each silent in the moment.

Finishing our drinks more hastily now but in silence, a feeling almost like a magnetic pull between us intensified, drawing us closer against the current of reason. A fleeting glance, a shared moment of understanding, and suddenly, we were consumed by a need that eclipsed our carefully crafted boundaries.

The allure was undeniable, the tension palpable as our lips met in a fervent embrace. His body was leaning into mine on the couch, bending me backwards as he shoved his tongue down my throat. This was not a goodbye kiss. Continuously as his lips locked with mine he struggled simultaneously to take off his flannel button down. Bodies tangled in a symphony of desire and familiarity, the lines between friendship and something deeper blurred in the haze of passion.

"Should we take this to the red room?" suggested Benji almost out of breath just from kissing me.

"I thought you were gonna leave?" I mocked him.

"You know I can't go anywhere without taking care of you, after all you are my favorite toy." I didn't know if he meant that he liked to play with me sexually or emotionally, it was probably both but the red flags of him being emotionally unavailable blurred as he grabbed me by the hair. "Get on your knees, follow me, crawl to bed."

Here I was, drooling on myself already, my jaw practically

on the ground in awe of how this man was able to put me in sub space so easily. Left, right, left, right, hands and knees on the ground crawling on all fours with him slightly ahead of me, still gripping my hair in his hands.

We reached the red room, he let go of my hair, and sat down on the edge of the bed. "Take off my pants" he demanded of me. Unbuttoning his jeans, slowly unzipping his fly, peeling the denim down his legs revealing a bulge in his briefs all for me. "Well, go on, open your mouth." he ordered as he lowered his briefs. I obeyed. "Look up at me" he said seconds before spitting down my throat.

The air was thick with anticipation as I watched him intently, my cheeks flushed with nerves and desire. I hesitated for a moment, my heart pounding against my rib cage, but I knew I couldn't back down now. I kept my mouth open, feeling his eyes on me. The anticipation was almost unbearable as he slowly fed his throbbing cock into my mouth. His hips gently rocked back and forth, as my mouth moved in rhythm with him. His hands gripped the back of my head, guiding me as I tasted his saltiness and the musky scent of his arousal. I could hear the sounds of his breathing becoming more ragged, and I knew I was pleasing him. His thrusts grew faster, and I clung to his hips for support. He groaned softly, his hips bucking harder as he reached the peak of his excitement.

The feeling of him using me as his own personal sex toy had me throbbing and dripping wet between my thighs. I didn't have any thoughts other than just being his hole. As he removed his cock from my throat, he bent forward slightly, placing both hands around the base of my neck and pulled and motioned for me to sit on the corner of the bed. On the edge of my seat, quite literally, his hands still around my neck, he slammed me into the mattress. My panties were absolutely dripping with my own secretion. He didn't even bother with taking them off, he just pulled them to the side with his right hand as his left was still around my neck.

I couldn't help but moan as his cock penetrated me with a quick and harsh thrust, sending waves of pleasure coursing through my body. The sound of our flesh slapping together filled the room, and I could feel the sweat trickling down my back as he pounded me harder and faster. His grip on my neck tightened, and I knew he was taking control of this encounter. My breasts bounced wildly with each impact, my nipples straining against the fabric of my bra. As I looked up at him, our eyes locked, and I could see the raw intensity in his gaze. He was not merely using me as a sex toy, but as an outlet for his deepest fantasies. I found myself lost in the moment, craving the release that only he could give me, and as he thrust into me, I knew that I would do anything to satisfy him, to make him feel as whole as possible.

"The only thing you're good for is being my obedient slut. You are my favorite toy." he proclaimed in a husky voice low right next to my ear as his whole body hovered slightly above mine as he continued to thrust deep inside of me. My hands gripped at the cotton sheets below me as Benji continued to use me and turn me into a fragile little broken thing.

His thrusts into me became faster and no longer in pattern. Suddenly I felt a brisk chill against my throat as he slammed his cock into me and held it there. I opened my eyes and realized he had pulled out his Bowie knife and had it against my skin. My heart raced, fear was coursing through my veins like ice, as I lay there pinned beneath him. The cold steel of the blade pressed against my tender neck, a stark reminder of the power he held over me. Benji's breathing filled the otherwise silent air, a symphony of lust and rage.

"Told you I'd make an example out of you, didn't I?" Benji whispered, his breath hot and heavy against my ear. The knife, cold and unyielding. I bit my lip, tears pricking at my eyes, helpless and trembling under his dominant touch. I couldn't deny the fear that gripped me, but there was something else, too. A strange mix of shame and arousal that seemed to be burning within me, as if the pain and humiliation only served to heighten my desire.

"Just like that, beg for your life, slut. Do it. Show me how much you crave my mercy." His voice was low and taunting, a dangerous game that I knew I shouldn't play. But my body betrayed me, betraying every ounce of my being. "Please, Benji, please fuck me more, please I crave your cock Daddy."

"Turn over, on your knees," he said, "keep your ass up." I shakily flipped over and before I could feel stable Benji's hands gripped at my waist and he was sliding himself right back inside of me. "I want you to cum for me, willingly or not."

I was able to maneuver placing my arm underneath my torso reaching for my clit. I was so wet, a sloppy mess of my own fluids. I rubbed myself out as Daddy continued to pummel me from behind, a knife still in his hands, harder and faster the more I moaned. "Moan for me, my sweet little toy." There it was, bliss, orgasm, screaming out in pleasure right as he filled me at the very same moment. Connection.

I practically fell over myself, laying down in the tousled sheets. Benji laid down next to me, picking me up slightly by the shoulders to have me lay on his chest. In the aftermath of really hot and kinky, but quick, sex, we nestled in the silence of the night, we lay entwined, the weight of my feelings lingering in the air like an unresolved melody. Feelings now growing stronger at a heavily connected hook up. The boundaries we clung to of just being casual felt like they were faltering. It felt like there was a truth to feelings on both parties being more than just casual sex that neither of us dared acknowledge. Maybe it was wishful thinking on my end, but the connection just felt so pure.

"You should stay." I tried to ask as casually as possible, looking up slightly and grabbing his hand within mine.

"No I should go, staying feels a little too serious, maybe it's better this way instead, we're just best together sexually and I don't want this to be anything more…" Benji mused, his voice a mere whisper in the night. He played with my hand in his hand before letting go and dropping it. "Plus I need to get some real sleep tonight. I have a really big day at work tomorrow, someone is coming in with this super intricate portrait tattoo they want and I need to be sharp for it."

I nodded, a silent agreement to bury the echoes of emotional pain this night beneath the facade of casual intimacy. As I watched Benji put on his shirt, a rush of conflicting emotions flooded me. His departure was inevitable, but I was rather hopeful it would be in the morning instead. I couldn't help but feel disappointment as reality nudged me.

My eyes traced the curve of his back as he moved around the red room, collecting his scattered belongings and clothing. Each movement emphasized more and more that he was leaving. Just moments ago we shared significant intimacy, now it all felt like a distant memory.

As he turned to me, a faint smile across his lips, but his eyes reflected the same inner turmoil I was feeling.

"I'll just go ahead and let myself out." he said before he turned towards the hallway. The sound of the front door closing behind him echoed in the silence, leaving me all alone in bed. He didn't even kiss me goodbye. I was convincing myself I was overthinking everything. I had to be. I need to stop spiraling, I was going to get myself hurt.

I lay there, my heart heavy with a mix of confusion and longing. The empty space beside me seemed to mock the moments we had just shared. Has it all been a facade? A temporary escape from reality? I couldn't shake off the feeling that I was missing something, that there was a hidden truth lurking beneath the surface. With a deep breath, I swung my legs over the edge of the bed and reached for my robe. As I tied the sash tightly around my waist, I felt a determination welling up inside me. I couldn't let myself be consumed by doubt and speculation any longer. If I wanted answers, I would have to seek them out myself.

I collected myself, turned off the lights downstairs, and headed up to my room to sneak between Alejandra and Jake in bed knowing that it wasn't good for my mental health to be alone right now. Even if they were asleep, I needed the aftercare of a human body's warmth next to mine after Benji left without giving me any. I mean, just moments ago a knife was at my throat.

The soft glow of moonlight filtered through the curtains as I slipped into bed, sandwiching myself between Alejandra and Jake. Their steady breathing and warmth provided a comforting respite for my weary soul. The events of the evening still echoed in my mind. In the calm darkness, memories of Benji's departure swirled tumultuously within me. His sudden exit had left an emotional void, a void that threatened to consume my fragile mind and heart.

Chapter 5: 9/8

I stood in front of the mirror, excitement within me like a fizzy soda that had been shaken up just waiting to burst. The vibrant hues of my wardrobe lay sprawled across the bed—a mini skirt, black cowboy boots, and that daring leopard print crop top I'd been saving just for this occasion is what I ended up deciding on. I got dressed and immediately was feeling a surge of confidence. I looked so good.

"Girl, you look absolutely fierce!" Alejandra exclaimed, entering the room with an amused sparkle in her eyes. She circled me, taking in the sassy yet playful look.

I twirled, relishing the swish of my skirt. "Thanks, babe! I'm channeling my inner rock star tonight."

"Well, let me add the finishing touch," Alejandra said, reaching for her makeup kit.

I was so thankful Alejandra was a girly girl because that was not me and doing makeup was not my thing.

"Voilà!" Alejandra announced, holding up a mirror for me to admire her work.

She gave me a perfect smoky eye look and a fiercely sharp wing, a challenge on my hooded eyes. "You're a magician, Alejandra! I feel like a goddess!"

With a quick kiss on Alejandra's lips, I grabbed my phone

and keys. Ingrid, my friend from college, awaited me outside. We were going to see a band we both loved tonight together and we hadn't spent time with each other in months.

"Girl, you're glowing! I've missed these outings with you," Ingrid exclaimed as I ran down the steps to my front door meeting up with her and linking arms.

"Tell me about it! Tonight's gonna be epic," I grinned, feeling a surge of nostalgia mixed with anticipation.

On the drive to the venue I found myself laughing, my cheeks hurting from the wide grin plastered on my face—a testament to the joy I felt being in Ingrid's company again.

The amphitheater loomed ahead, vibrant lights against the night sky with a distant hum of the crowd's excitement.

We entered the venue, and wove our way closer to the stage, surrendering ourselves to the euphoria of the music.

In the midst of the energy, my mind drifted momentarily to Benji—I found myself searching for an excuse to bring him up to Ingrid and talk about him. But I dared not show my new relationship energy because I knew it would just come across as obnoxious and annoying. But he's all I could think about as the band played a harmonious love song. Fuck I was down bad for this man. The longer I went without seeing him, the more I thought about him. I hadn't heard from him since the other night and wanted to talk to him about so much.

As the music pulsed through my veins, I couldn't help but feel an ache in my chest. The lyrics of the song intertwined with my longing for Benji, creating a bittersweet symphony within me. The melody became a backdrop to the memories we had created together, a soundtrack to the moments we had shared. Ingrid, sensing my distraction, leaned closer and shouted over the booming speakers, "What's on your mind? You seem lost in another world."

I smiled weakly, trying to regain my composure. "It's nothing," I replied, my voice barely audible above the crowd. "Just caught up in the music."

Ingrid's eyes narrowed slightly, uncertainty etched across her face. She had always been able to sense when something was bothering me. We had been friends for years, and she knew me better than anyone else. But this time, I couldn't bring myself to confide in her. She would definitely think that Benji was a walking red flag. She wasn't going to understand my obsession with a man that held a knife to me during sex.

Hours slipped away, the concert coming to a close, both myself and Ingrid high on adrenaline and a little tipsy. The exhilaration of the concert lingered, as we headed home.

The night had brought us closer, I started to think maybe I should just tell her about Benji. After all, she's the closest person I have to being a best friend. Maybe she'd have some insight.

We got into the car and began our drive back to my house where we had originally met up. Ingrid could clearly sense I was being unusually quiet. "Everything okay?" she asked, her voice gentle as she glanced at me from the passenger seat.

"Yea, there's just this guy, his name is Benji."

"There's always some guy, do Jake and Alejandra know about him?"

"Yea they do, all three of us have kind of gotten entangled in his life a bit. I don't know, he's different, he's charismatic, captivating, but I just think you will assume he might just be bad news."

Ingrid's eyebrows rose in surprise, "Bad news? How so?"

I sighed, my eyes fixed on the road ahead. "It's hard to

explain," I began, my voice tinged with uncertainty. "There's something about him, Ingrid. He's got this mysterious aura that draws people in, but—I can't shake the feeling that he's hiding something. Like he's carrying a darkness within him. But he feels so perfect. He just tells me one thing and his body language says the opposite."

Ingrid leaned back in her seat, contemplating my words. "And you think this darkness could affect you and your friends?"

I nodded, my grip on the steering wheel tightening. "Exactly. Jake, Alejandra, and I have found ourselves caught up in his life and I'm absolutely in his web of secrets. He has this way of weaving himself into MY life, making it difficult to distance myself. If I'm being honest I am absolutely falling for him."

Silence hung in the air for a moment before Ingrid finally spoke. "Well, if you suspect he might be bad news, maybe it's best to keep your guard up."

"I'm trying," I admitted, my voice laced with frustration.

As we approached home, I hopped out of my car and gave Ingrid a hug goodbye, "This was such a good night, I wish we could keep the party going but I unfortunately work in the morning," Ingrid exclaimed. "Sometime soon though let's not go this long without seeing each other again! And you better keep me posted on Benji and how that all plays out." I nodded in agreement, a smile playing at the corners of my lips. Ingrid's words resonated with me, as I too realized how much I had missed our time together.

Looking down at my phone, I saw the time was only ten o'clock. It was a Friday. The night was young. I fiddled with my keys and opened the front door, pitch black welcomed me. Alejandra and Jake must already be in bed. Fuck I loved them but they were such introverts and total sleepy heads.

I turned on the foyer light, kicked off my boots, and walked downstairs to settle in on the couch. I pulled out my phone and stared at it. Should I?

"Hey Benji, how's your night going? Getting into anything?" Hitting send quickly before I could second guess myself. Maybe he was bad news, but I absolutely loved getting into trouble.

Ping! An immediate text back.

"No actually, I was thinking about grabbing a drink at the dive bar near my house, would you want to meet up there?"

It seemed like a rare opportunity that he wanted to go out with me in public. I jumped up off the couch, grabbing a red bull out of my fridge and shoving my cowboy boots back on my feet.

"Yea which bar? Send the address and I'll meet you there!"

He wanted to meet up at Northside Lounge, a dive I was familiar with but didn't know that was close to his house because he had never brought me over before. We always hung out at my house. I typed the location into my phone's GPS and headed right back out the door despite just getting home 10 minutes prior and was on my way.

I shot a text to the group chat since my partners were home but asleep. "Hey guys Benji and I are meeting up for a drink. The concert with Ingrid was a good time! Will keep you posted!"

As I pulled up to the bar and parallel parked my car, my heart was racing with anxiety. How do I act with Benji in public? Can I kiss him? Am I a secret? What are we even doing?

The dimly lit ambiance of Northside Lounge enveloped me as I pushed through the heavy wooden door. A wave of nervous energy in my chest grew with each step I took. Tonight was different—meeting Benji here felt like stepping into uncharted territory.

I immediately spotted Benji at a corner table, our eyes met instantly and he waved at me, a half-smile gracing his lips, beckoning me to join him.

"Hey, Callie!" Benji greeted me with a casual nod as I slid into the seat across from him.

"Hi, Benji," my voice was slightly more jittery than usual. I fidgeted with the coaster on the table, unsure of how to navigate a public interaction with Benji. I needed a double shot stat.

A brief awkward silence hung between us before Benji cleared his throat. "What are you drinking tonight? Let me pick up your first round!"

"Um, a gin and tonic, I guess," I responded, feeling a surge of relief at the familiar comfort of alcohol as a social lubricant. "I started with gin tonight at a concert earlier so it's probably a safe bet to stick with that."

"Oh yea? A concert? Who'd you go see?"

Finally, a conversation that flowed easily, easing the awkwardness of our public encounter. We chatted for a while after the bartender brought us our round of drinks. I told him about the concert I went to, my friend Ingrid, and answered some more of his questions about my lifestyle generally.

"Hey we'll close out when ya get a minute!" Benji motioned at the bartender before I was even done with my first drink.

"Let's take a walk," Benji suggested suddenly, "My place is just around the corner!"

I nodded in agreement, welcoming the opportunity to be away from the prying eyes that made me feel unusually self-conscious. This was enough public interaction for me for one evening with Benji. I wanted to settle into the familiarity of what we usually do together.

63

The cool night air washed over us as we strolled along the block, the distant sounds of the bar fading into the background. My nerves slowly settled the further we walked.

"I live just a couple of blocks away," Benji mentioned again casually, a glint of invitation in his eyes.

My curiosity piqued at his subtle invitation. The idea of exploring his world, the place he called home, enticed me. With a gentle smile, I accepted the offer, eager for the chance to deepen our connection.

We left the bar together after closing out and headed down the street. As we turned the corner, the city noises melted away, replaced by a tranquil ambiance. The streets became quieter, the buildings more residential. Softly glowing street lights wrapped us in a warm embrace as we walked hand in hand. Benji's pace slowed, allowing me time to take in the details of his neighborhood.

We arrived at Benji's doorstep, "I think I've told you before but I live with Chad right now, he's not home but his dog is here so I hope that's okay." He unlocked the door, ushering me inside with a reassuring smile. We walked down a hallway, and he opened the last door on the left. The space felt intimate yet foreign—a glimpse into Benji's private world.

The room was dimly lit, the wooden floor was worn. I stepped inside cautiously, feeling like a trespasser in this intimate sanctuary. The air was heavy with the scent of old books. As my eyes adjusted to the darkness, I could make out the shelves that lined the walls, sagging under the weight of countless volumes. Benji's love for literature was evident in every corner of the room. The shelves were filled with an eclectic mix of genres - classic novels, poetry collections, and modern works. It was as if each book had its own story to tell, waiting patiently for a pair of curious eyes to stumble upon it. I traced my fingers along the spines, feeling a sense of reverence for these pages that held infinite worlds within their covers. Benji watched me, his eyes gleaming with anticipation. "I've always found solace in books," he said as I continued to look at the selection he had.

Benji's words hung in the air, lingering between us like a delicate thread connecting our hearts. With every passing moment, that thread pulled tighter, entangling us in a web of emotions we had both tried to suppress. I knew he was charismatic, but now I better understood why.

He offered me another drink, and we settled on his bed, tension simmering between us.

"I like having you here, Callie," he admitted softly, his eyes searching mine. "I can't believe I've never brought you over here before."

"I've always wanted this," I confessed, my voice barely above a whisper. "But it's complicated, isn't it?"

He nodded, his gaze never leaving mine. "It is. We've spent some time now both tiptoeing around our feelings, afraid of what might happen if we let them run free."

I felt a rush of emotions—vulnerability mingled with desire, a longing for connection, and a fear of crossing lines we had carefully navigated. Yet, there was an undeniable pull—a magnetic force drawing me closer to Benji.

He sat up, leaned over me, and placed his drink on the bedside table. In one swift movement he grabbed my drink out of my hands, and placed it next to his on the table as well. His hand met my jaw, grabbing at my face delicately, as our lips met in a quick subtle embrace. Everything I thought I understood about the situation felt different. Benji was being sweet, a little romantic even.

My hands now followed his to take charge of the situation, one hand at my waist, one still delicately on my face. I took my hands and now grabbed onto his, moving them lower to the hem of my skirt.

"Are you trying to take this off of me?" I said to him in a coy playful manner.

Without hesitation his hands pulled down my skirt, grabbed at my shirt and pulled that up and over my head. He placed his weight on top of me, still fully dressed himself, and began kissing me intensely. I had my hands around his face as he kissed me more and more, me naked and quivering below him. Benji was moaning ever so slightly as his body pressed into mine and our lips continued to meet.

His left hand traveled south, flicking at my pussy just a touch. "You're so wet," he said right before taking both of my wrists in one of his hands and holding them above my head. "I can sense how bad you want me, my sweet pet."

His hands let go of my wrists, he took off his shirt hastily, unbuttoned his jeans, peeled them off of his body and was right back to holding my hands together above my head and biting at my neck. "You want me so bad I think I'm going to tease you a bit more though kitten."

He looked into my eyes, almost as if he was expecting me to protest him, but I just went along with the little game he wanted to play.

"God, you're just so beautiful," he whispered in my ear.

He moved down between my legs and quickly slid himself inside of me, rock hard and pulsing. Benji started thrusting slowly, which was a little surprising considering how rough he usually is.

"Faster Benji, fuck, please!" He obeyed the orders immediately, pumping his cock deep inside of me. His one hand was still holding my wrists together above my head, and the faster he fucked me, the harder he held on. I was certain there would be bruises there later on. After all, I loved when he marked me as his. It was on my list of things to do to go get a tattoo from him so I could feel permanently marked by him.

Benji kept thrusting into me, his thrusts getting sloppier, a sure sign that he was close to cumming. I felt his cock twitch inside of me. "Benji" I said breathing more heavily now, feeling my orgasm build up as well. "Fuck Benji" he kept thrusting into me.

He pulled out almost all of the way and then slammed back into me as hard as he could causing us both to hit a euphoric high of orgasm. I felt him fill me. I squeezed the inside of my walls like I do with kegels, milking everything I could out of his cock. He pulled out, rolled off of me, and laid beside me in silence allowing us both to just catch our breathe.

"What do you want to do now?" Benji asked.

"Well, I guess I'm going to finish my drink and head home?"

Heading home seemed the most logical, I got my hookup and came, he got his, we were not together, time to go right?

"Why don't you stay here tonight, I can give you a big t-shirt of mine to sleep in so we can drink some more and maybe watch a movie or something?"

I lay there, a tangle of sheets and emotions, as Benji's words hung in the air like an unexpected melody. "Stay the night?" I repeated, my voice a mixture of surprise and curiosity. My eyes traced the contours of Benji's face, searching for an indication of what prompted this change. He looked back at me, his expression unreadable, yet there was a softness in his eyes that I hadn't noticed before.

Making my decision, I nodded slowly. "Okay, I'll stay."

The rest of the evening passed in a blur of new discoveries. We talked, really talked, for what felt like the first time ever.

As I lay beside him, my head resting on his chest, listening to the steady rhythm of his heart, I felt a confusing mix of emotions. There was comfort in his warmth, a sense of belonging that I hadn't anticipated. But there was also fear, a nagging worry that this newfound intimacy might shatter the fragile balance of our relationship.

Morning arrived with a soft light filtering through the curtains, casting a gentle glow across the room. I stirred awake, aware of Benji's presence beside me. Our eyes met, and for a moment, there was a silent communication, an understanding that something had shifted between the two of us.

"Hey I gotta head home, but, I'll see you this weekend yea? Alejandra's birthday party?"

"Absolutely, I wouldn't miss it for the world. Thanks for staying last night, it was nice to not be alone.

As I left, my mind was a whirlwind of thoughts. I needed time to think, to understand what this change meant for us. Was this the beginning of something more, or was it just a beautiful anomaly in our casual affair?

Chapter 6: 9/16

The basement was a hive of activity. Today was not just any day; it was Alejandra's birthday, and I was determined to make it unforgettable.

As I maneuvered through stacks of decorations and party supplies, I couldn't help but feel a flutter of excitement mixed with nerves. I wanted everything to be perfect for my girlfriend, who had no idea about the surprise awaiting her later that evening. She was out to dinner with her parents, she knew she was coming home to a party, keeping a surprise from her was difficult, but she didn't know what all I was setting up or how many people were coming.

In one corner of the basement, I set up a photo booth, complete with a backdrop of shimmering curtains and a table full of quirky props. I envisioned the guests taking silly photos, capturing memories that would last a lifetime. In the garage I set up a beer pong table. I set up a snack table adorned with a luxurious red velvet tablecloth, in the middle, a punch bowl cocktail. I scattered around a few vases, in them were Alejandra's favorite flowers – vibrant tulips and daisies. As I adjusted the placement of the cutlery, my mind wandered to Alejandra's reaction. I could almost see her, walking down the stairs, her eyes wide with surprise and delight. I smiled to herself, feeling a surge of love and anticipation.

Turning my attention back to the food, I checked the array of dishes laid out on a separate table. Yes, she was at dinner with her family, but it seemed in poor taste to have a party with alcohol and not have any snacks. There were Alejandra's favorites – spicy empanadas, homemade guacamole, and a rich chocolate cake waiting to be unveiled at the right moment. I had spent the previous night baking the cake, determined to get it just right. It was a three-layered masterpiece, covered in smooth chocolate ganache and decorated with edible gold leaf. It was more than just a cake; it was a labor of love. The bar was stocked with an array of beverages, from fine wines to craft beers and every type of liquor possible. Like I said, our space was designed to host.

With most of the setup complete, I took a moment to breathe. I decided to text Benji, "Hey can't wait to see you tonight." Everything was ready, just as I had planned.

I had pulled it off – the perfect birthday party for Alejandra.

The clock ticked closer to the time the guests were due to arrive. I took one final look around, ensuring everything was in place. The lights, the music, the food, it all came together so perfectly. I glanced at my watch. Any minute now, the first of the guests would start arriving.

As the first guests began to arrive, I greeted them with a bright smile and a welcome drink. I watched as the basement slowly filled with people, laughter, and conversation. Friends and colleagues of Alejandra's mingled while I just kept scanning the crowd for Benji. My heart raced every time a new guest arrived, hoping to see Benji.

Alejandra had come home from dinner and was welcomed warmly by all of her friends, she was absolutely the center of attention, her infectious laughter echoing through the basement. She looked radiant, and my heart swelled with affection as I watched my girlfriend enjoying her special day.

However, the absence of Benji was becoming increasingly noticeable. I checked my phone constantly, but there was no message from him. I tried to focus on the guests and the party, but a part of my mind was occupied with thoughts of him. Was he going to surprise me by showing up late? Did something come up?

The party was in full swing, the air filled with the melody of happy conversations and music, when my phone buzzed. My heart leapt as I pulled out my phone, but my excitement quickly turned to disappointment. It was a text from Benji.

"Hey Callie, I'm so sorry but I can't make it tonight. Something came up. I hope you guys have a great time. Say Happy Birthday to Alejandra from me."

I stared at the message, feeling a mix of sadness and understanding. Life was unpredictable, and things happened, but I couldn't help feeling a little heartbroken. Taking a deep breath, I composed myself and replied, "No worries, Benji. Thanks for letting me know. We'll miss you."

Putting my phone away, I looked around at the party. The house was alive with joy and celebration, and I realized that despite Benji's absence, it was a beautiful night. I made my way to Alejandra, who was laughing at a joke someone had just told.

"Everything okay?" Alejandra asked.

I smiled, nodding. "Yeah, everything's perfect. Just got a message from Benji, he can't make it."

Alejandra wrapped an arm around my waist, a reassuring squeeze. "Well, we have a home full of amazing people who did make it. Let's enjoy the party, my love."

She was right. The night was about celebrating Alejandra. Life was full of unexpected turns, but it was also full of moments like these, moments of love, friendship, and joy. And for now, that was all that mattered.

The evening continued to unfold beautifully. The music blended seamlessly into the background. My disappointment was tucked away, as I immersed myself in the festivities. I moved through the crowd, chatting and laughing, making sure everyone had a drink and was enjoying themselves.

Alejandra danced with friends, shared stories, and radiated happiness. As I sunk into the corner with introverted Jake, we just watched her together, both feeling a deep sense of love and admiration. This was the woman we had chosen to be with, and every day she reminded us of how right that decision was.

"You did a great job on the party babe," encouraged Jake, "seriously, look at her she's so happy, I'm sorry Benji did not show but tonight is still going to be an incredible night."

As the night drew on, the atmosphere remained light and joyful. People gathered in small groups, some dancing, others engaged in deep conversation. The table with snacks and drinks was always surrounded by a cluster of guests.

Eventually, the party reached its natural peak, and guests began to say their goodbyes. Myself, Jake, and Alejandra stood together at the door, thanking everyone for coming and sharing in the celebration. Once the last guest had left, we all turned to each other knowing where the evening was about to go.

Alejandra wrapped her arms around me, pulling me in close. "Thank you for tonight, love. It was perfect."

"I'm just glad you enjoyed it. That's all that matters."

Alejandra looked up at me with a thoughtful expression. "Hey, I was thinking," she began, "since Benji couldn't make it tonight, why don't we invite him over for dinner tomorrow? It might be nice, a more relaxed setting to catch up."

I was taken aback by the suggestion. "That's a lovely idea," I replied, "I'll message him in the morning and see if he's free."

Alejandra smiled, pleased. "Great! It'll be fun. So, what do you two have in store for the birthday girl for the rest of the night?"

"Night?" Jake said with a chuckle, "it's three in the morning babe, but don't worry, we're not letting the birthday girl go to bed without some birthday sex..."

I blushed, feeling a surge of excitement at Jake's suggestion. "Oh, I think we can definitely make that happen," I replied with a mischievous grin. Alejandra laughed and playfully nudged me. "Well then, let's not waste any more time. Lead the way."

We made our way upstairs to our bedroom, hand in hand. We all laid down in bed together, and me and Jake immediately began undressing the birthday girl. Jake pulled her underwear off and her dress off as I went in for a kiss. The moment our lips touched, Alejandra's deep brown eyes fluttered shut, her long lashes forming a delicate fan against her cheeks. I could see the subtle movements of her lips as she parted them, inviting me in for a deeper kiss.

She started to struggle to kiss me back as I realized Jake was already busy going down on her. I went in for her neck and began marking her. I reveled in the taste of her skin. Every kiss and gentle graze of my teeth against her neck magnified the intensity of our connection. She responded eagerly to my touch, her soft moans urging me further. Her fingers danced across my back, tracing fiery paths that ignited my passion.

She gasped and squirmed beneath me, her eyes wide with desire and a hint of fear as I continued to leave marks on her neck, and moved lower to her breasts as Jake continued to eat her out. I traced the curve of her breasts with my lips, feeling the subtle quiver under my touch. I wanted to savor every moment with her, to make this night unforgettable.

I pulled away, catching my breath while absently tracing the delicate line of her collarbone. Her fingers found their way to my hair, gently tugging, urging me closer. I leaned in, our lips meeting in a fervent kiss. The heat from her body seemed to radiate through the three of us in the moment.

I continued to kiss her as Jake stopped eating her out, he looked up at us enjoying our moment of passion. That was when he grabbed at her waist and pulled her lower, closer to him.

She moaned softly, her body arching against me as Jake expertly positioned her with a gentle tug on her hips. I could feel the unmistakable build-up of her so close to orgasm already, the way her body was responding to our combined efforts, and the sweat that gathered on our skin from the intense, erotic embrace we were sharing.

As Jake continued to move in sync with her body, thrusting himself deeper inside of her as I helped by toying with her clit and pulling at her hair. Her breaths became more labored, each one mingling with the soft moans escaping her lips. I could see the anticipation in her eyes, the raw desire and intensity growing with every passing moment. I pulled her hair harder. Suddenly, she let out a loud cry, her entire body trembling as she reached the peak of her pleasure.

The sight of her writhing beneath Jake sent my own desire spiraling, and I knew that it was only a matter of time before I too would find my release. Our bodies were now slick with sweat and the mingled scent of our arousal filled the air.

The room buzzed with anticipation as our breaths became ragged, each one more intense than the last. My eyes locked with Jake's, and I could see the same hunger that raged within him, mirrored in mine.

"Well the birthday girl seems spent," Jake muttered softly. "I think Callie deserves some too for all the work she did today setting up the party."

The weight of desire became too great, too overwhelming. I knew I couldn't hold back any longer, suddenly Jake's hand snaked between my legs, he found the entrance of my core and pushed his fingers deep inside of me.

"Babe, you want another birthday treat? Wanna help me with her?" He suggested Alejandra motioning towards the two of them using me together. Alejandra smiled mischievously, her eyes sparkling with playful anticipation. "Oh, I'd love to," she replied, her voice laced with excitement. She inched closer to me on the bed, her fingers gently tracing the outline of my body as if mapping out a secret path.

As her fingers moved across my skin, I couldn't help but feel a thrill run through me. Alejandra's touch was unlike anything I'd ever experienced before. I rounded my eyes and shivered, instinctively arching my hips towards her. She gave me a sly grin, her eyes locked onto mine, as she slowly leaned in to brush her lips against my inner thigh. The warmth of her breath and the softness of her lips sent my world into a tailspin. Her tongue darted between the lips between my legs.

She raised her head and whispered, "Are you ready for what's next, my love?" I could barely utter a word, my mind lost in a haze of desire for her. All I could manage was a nod. Jake then positioned himself to grab at my hips, pulling me towards him, and thrusting himself deep inside of me, all the while Alejandra had herself delicately positioned to sit on my face, grinding into me, and using her fingers on my clit as Jake continued to rail me.

I moaned softly, my body shuddering with each thrust from Jake. I could feel the intensity of Alejandra's touch as her fingers danced over my sensitive nerves. My mind was a whirlwind of pleasure, every sensation heightened by the passion surrounding me. Jake's rhythm was unrelenting, his body slamming against mine with a desperation that matched my own. I could feel Alejandra's hips grinding harder, her movements in sync with Jake's. Her moans echoed the sound of our lovemaking. I could barely keep up with the overwhelming sensations, as Alejandra's juices slid down my face.

My moans became louder, more urgent, as I felt the sweet agony of climax building within me. A flood of ecstasy coursed through my veins. My body arched, my breath ragged. Every muscle in my body tensed, then relaxed. As I lay there, panting and spent, I felt as though I had just experienced a small piece of heaven itself. In that moment of pure sensuality, all worries and cares dissolved.

I closed my eyes and savored the afterglow, knowing that I had just shared something truly magical with my two loving partners. We lay together, our hearts beating in unison.

"Well, that sure was a fantastic birthday." Alejandra whispered, her voice hoarse, "the party was good too!"

Jake and I both chuckled. "I am so glad you had a good night sweetheart, I think I speak for both me and Jake when I say we did too!"

As the room filled with the warm glow of moonlight, Alejandra's tired eyes sparkled with affectionate gratitude. She reached out, her right hand fingertips brushing against Jake's hand, and then gently entwined the fingers of her other hand with mine. As a trio there was a shared post sex tender smile and we all began to drift asleep.

Chapter 7: 10/6

Part One

People think I'm a slut because I'm bisexual, polyamorous, and in a throuple. They're absolutely right but it's a bit presumptive. Well, how's that phrase go, if the shoe fits wear it? It's October 6th, National Kink Day in the states, and as a throuple we annually throw a party for the day, well, an orgy of sorts. What better day to have an orgy you know? It was mainly my idea being the extroverted most horny one of the trio but Alejandra and Jake were just as excited as me, and both had their fair share of inviting friends and crushes.

All of our closest friends were invited, pretty much anyone was welcome, but only the bravest RSVP'd.

I invited Benji and his best friend Chad, mainly to be polite, but I highly doubted either of them would come. Besides, everyone I knew that was actually coming was queer. Benji and Chad were unfortunately very straight. I feared if they did come they'd be rather uncomfortable.

The morning was full of chores, making sure all the bar ware was clean, the floors were mopped, blankets were washed. We'd hosted an orgy or two before and had a whole set-up planned. The downstairs was the sex space, I mean of course we had the infamous red room, and in the living room between the two couches we moved the coffee table and plopped our king size mattress in the middle on the floor. Watching three of us carry it down a flight of stairs was interesting to say the least but, you do what you have to do.

I began to light incense in every corner of the downstairs main room and red room to clear the air. There was a thin wisp of smoke curls from the end of the incense sticks, twisting and swirling like a dancer in the air. The scent of sandalwood and patchouli permeated the room.

As the clock ticked closer to the evening, the energy in the house began to buzz with anticipation. The scent of incense continued to fill the air, creating an atmosphere of sensuality and desire. Alejandra, Jake, and I double-checked everything, ensuring that every detail was perfect for our guests. Tonight was more than just a celebration of kinks; it was a celebration of love, freedom, queerness, and exploration.

I couldn't help but feel a pang of curiosity about whether Benji and Chad would show up. It wasn't so much about their potential discomfort; it was more about witnessing their reaction to an environment so radically different from what they were used to. The thought fascinated me. In my experience, pushing boundaries often led to unexpected growth and understanding.

Right then, a ping from my phone. The text was from Benji, "Hey, are there gonna be finger sandwiches at the orgy party tonight?" I couldn't tell if he was being funny, or rather I should say, punny, or if he was genuinely asking because he was planning on coming.

"Haha, yes there will be snacks, even though I'm a whole snack myself thank you very much." I responded back quickly.

"No finger sandwiches, no cum."

"Daddy, I need your cum to be the sauce for the finger sandwiches actually, at least mine."

"Haha" his response was short. I truly could not tell if he was being funny or serious.

"Okay well as a matter of fact there will be finger sandwiches so, see you tonight?" I inquired.

"We shall see, Chad and I might show up just to watch. How many people are going to be there or participate?"

I wracked my brain for an answer, "Mmm, like 12 or so people?"

"Okay cool, exciting, I will be there, probably overwhelmed in the corner."

I couldn't even begin to imagine what it looked like for Benji to be overwhelmed. He was so cool and charismatic and always blended in so nice. Him in a corner overwhelmed and non verbal seemed off but I guess not everyone is as calm and collected with group sex as I am. After all, my living arrangement is an everyday threesome.

"It's okay if you're overwhelmed and don't want to participate," I said, "but you know I've been so very desperate for your cock again and your hand across my face."

"I'm sure you're going to get plenty of cock tonight, you don't need mine."

"While I am taking someone else's cock, just know I'll be thinking about the fact that none of it is as satisfying to me as much as you." I hit send and put my phone back down thinking I was going to have the last word. My phone buzzed again, and I saw it was Benji. I opened the message with a curious smile.

"Wow, you sure know how to make a guy feel desired, I can't believe you're not even trying to get me to come over now," he wrote.

"Well, I did say you were welcome to join. Don't make me beg, though. The thought of your hands on me is enough to make me forget about the others. Just know, tonight, I will be wearing your scent, your touch, your mark upon me, even if you're being a wallflower. I am going to try to get you to play with me every chance I get. Is that enough for you?" I replied, my breath quickening at the thought of him there with me.

"Fine, fine, I'll show up for real. If I participate it'll only be with you. What time should I get there again?" he asked.

"We're starting around 8 o'clock, but feel free to come earlier if you want."

As the guests began to arrive, they entered through the front door and were greeted by the sight of the living room with the mattress on the ground, and down the hallway, the infamous red room, where all the kinky action would take place. The living room was the melting pot of the party, where people could mingle, make out, and even start exploring each other. There was a huge table in the corner of the room, laden with drinks, snacks, and of course the finger sandwiches.

Chad and Benji were among the first to show up. Both of them were dressed casually but fashionably, as if they had planned to come to an upscale dinner party rather than an explicit orgy. I watched nervously as they surveyed the room, taking in the sight of our throuple giving tours of the red room and the myriad of colorful people scattered across the floor.

Benji quickly made his way to me, his eyes twinkling with amusement. "So, where are the finger sandwiches at? I'm getting hangry." I chuckled and pointed to the snack table, where I had placed an array of food that could pass as finger food. "There you go, I made sure we had them, gotta keep my Daddy happy." I could see Benji's eyes lit up at the sight of the food, grinning from ear to ear.

The final guests arrived, everyone looked so phenomenal. I was wearing my best red lingerie. The halter bralette hugged my curves perfectly, accentuating my smaller but shapely C cup breasts. The bottoms were low rise, revealing a tantalizing glimpse of my smooth hips and the gem dangling just above my butt added a touch of elegance. Alejandra was wearing a leopard print vintage nightie. It nicely showed off Alejandra's toned arms and shoulders. Jake kept it simple, he wore some silky black boxers, and a furry red night robe that resembled something Hugh Hefner himself would wear around the Playboy mansion.

I approached the awkward duo, Chad and Benji at the snack table, sauntering over in my lingerie. "Hey, come meet everyone. We're gonna go over a boundary chat," I said, grinning. Benji raised an eyebrow, smirking. "Oh, okay," he said dryly, nodding towards the guests. He was very clearly out of his comfort zone.

I sat down on one of the couches, Jake on my left, and motioned Benji to sit on the other side of me. Chad stood next to him. "Welcome everyone, happy kink day!" I said as everyone hushed and listened to me. "We're going to get started here in a minute, but first we're going to go around the room and introduce ourselves. Please state your name, pronouns, sexuality, if you're comfortable playing with all genders or not, and what you're hoping to experience tonight."

I began the introductions, starting with myself. "My name is Callie, I use she/her pronouns, welcome to my house, I am bisexual, I play with all genders, I was recently tested for this event, and I am just hoping for a good time tonight however it pans out for me."

We went in a circle, so Jake was up next. "My name is Jake, and my pronouns are he/him. I'm a queer male, my partners here are Callie and Alejandra. As most of you know, I'm open to playing with all genders but I am hoping to experience some heavy sensation, play, and domination if possible with people of the same sex tonight."

Alejandra went next. "My name is Alejandra, and my pronouns are she/her. I'm a bisexual female, and I'm open to playing with all genders. I'm hoping to explore submission and submission play, as well as exhibitionism."

Dalton was next, a close friend to the throuple, stating more of the same, queer, open to everyone, looking for a good time. Then it was Ariel, a gal friend of ours we had met out at the gay bar recently. She stated she was only comfortable playing with the same sex. Nick and Samantha showed up, a couple that were friends with Alejandra and were wanting to explore polyamory more. And then there was Max and Jess, a married couple I was friends with that were already polyamorous but newer to the kink scene.

Next in the circle was Noah. They are a non-binary rigger. Noah started to speak, a look of quiet confidence filling their face. "I go by they/them pronouns. I'm queer and open to all genders. I'm a rigger, so I'm here to provide bondage and restraints for those who may be interested. I'm looking forward to exploring new dynamics and pushing boundaries tonight. I am more interested in providing kink than having sex. Anyone that wishes to be tied we'll be having one on one conversations for safety before I put you in my rope."

It was time to officially include nervous Chad and Benji in the festivities, as they were up next and last for introductions.

"I'm Chad, I use he/him pronouns, I'm a straight male, up for trying anything but mostly here for Callie, and hoping to just watch and learn from my surroundings," he said, visibly more nervous than before. "I'm open to trying new things, but I'm also a little nervous and I mainly came to just watch but not against participating if that's how things go. Just trying to go with the flow."

Last by not least, Benji's turn finally arrived. He took a deep breath and began to speak. "My name is Benji, and I go by he/him pronouns. I'm a straight male, but I'm here to support and be open to everyone. I'm actually quite nervous, but I know I can trust Callie and the rest of you." Once charismatic Benji was lost for words. "If I do play with anyone, it'll probably just be Callie as we've kinda been seeing each other and I am most comfortable with her. I'm still open to meeting new people and experiencing their kinks. I just need some time to acclimate to the situation."

"Alright everyone, thank you for your openness and honesty. Let's get started!" I proclaimed, and the kink day orgy was officially underway. Benji and Chad took a seat on a nearby couch, watching the action unfold around them with a mixture of intrigue and apprehension. Alejandra and Jake, wearing satisfied smiles, started exploring the room, engaging with different partners and discussions, while Noah stood by the staircase with their rope bag, waiting for their next adventurous kinkster.

Part Two

The start of an orgy is always a little awkward. Who's going to be the eager one to kick things off? Will people follow suit or do they need some more liquid confidence before diving in? Everyone knew I wasn't shy to play. I was the one hosting an orgy after all. I called Jess and Max over and asked Jess to lay down on the mattress that was on the ground. Our throuple had been friends with this couple for a while but we'd surprisingly never played together before and I really wanted to taste Jess. I also really wanted to put on a show for Benji.

Jess lay on her back, shyly still wearing a lacey purple bodysuit. "Let's get a little more comfortable, shall we?" I said as I slipped my finger under a shoulder strap. "Hey Max, wanna give me a hand here?" I motioned for him and he mimicked me lowering the shoulder strap of the bodysuit on the other side now. Through our teamwork, we pulled down the lingerie to reveal her gorgeous and large sized breasts.

We didn't waste any more time. Max and I together began to explore Jess's body. My fingers traced the outline of her vulva, teasing her just slightly, Max began kissing his partner just the way she liked which helped ease her in this newfound situation.

"Oh this looks like some fun I wanna join!" said Alejandra, climbing onto the mattress and immediately burying her face between Jess's legs. At that moment I realized I could stay and play in the little foursome that I created, or I could leave them to a little threesome and go check on Benji or get some other play started with some of the other guests.

I gave Jess a kiss, but between her partner Max and my partner Alejandra, she was in good hands and off to a good start. I got up and moved my way through the crowd of folks watching and mingling to talk to Benji. Naturally, he was back at the snack table.

"Do you want to play with me yet?" I asked so surely that he would change his mind on just watching.

"Maybe later, I'm enjoying watching you right now harness the night's energy."

I wasn't going to waste my night arguing with him so I ventured to see what was happening in the red room since some of the folks meandered their way down the hall. Upon entrance to the red room, I saw Noah weaving jute rope through Samantha's wrists, tying her to the bedpost. Her partner Nick was standing behind her with a leather bound flogger in hand. The intricate patterns of the knots in the shibari work accentuated Samantha's vulnerability, her body exposed and ready to be ravished. The flogger dangled from Nick's hand, its tails teasingly grazing Samantha's bare flesh. She winced periodically as the flogger impacted her bare bottom, but also as Noah pulled tight on the ropes around her wrists. A kinky little shibari threesome.

Looking back down the hall I was able to see a handful of people watching as Jake got involved with Max, Jess, and Alejandra, and was fully railing Jess while she was on all fours, sucking Max's dick as she took constant thrusts from Jake. I love my life. The fact that this was a Friday night in my own home was just incredible.

As the night went on, the heat in the red room intensified, both literally and emotionally. Every move and whisper echoed through the room. It seemed like everyone was having the time of their lives, each person lost in their own little world. The air was thick with anticipation, and I could feel my own desires flaring up within me. Benji approached me, "This is absolutely wild," he said with stars in his eyes. "Would it be weird if I asked Noah to tie me up? Shibari is something I have never experienced before and this seems like a safe space to do so."

"Wow, yea, absolutely, sorry I thought you weren't going to participate so asking about being tied up caught me off guard. Go ask them! They'd love to show you the ropes, quite literally."

I watched as Benji made his way towards Noah, his steps filled with nervous excitement. The dim, red lighting cast a sultry glow on their figures, heightening the intensity of the moment. As Benji approached, Noah turned, a mischievous smile playing on their lips. "Hey," Benji greeted, his voice tinged with anticipation. "I was wondering if you'd be up to tie me?" Noah's eyes sparkled with delight. "I'd be honored," they replied, gesturing for Benji to follow them to a secluded corner of the red room. The pair disappeared into the shadows, leaving me to observe from a distance. I couldn't help but be drawn to their intimate exchange as Noah began explaining the art of shibari to Benji. With every word and gesture, they wove in trust and connection.

As the ropes were carefully wrapped around Benji's body, I found myself staring and getting lost in my thoughts, I felt a gentle touch on my arm. Turning to face whoever touched me, I found myself looking into the piercing blue eyes of Ariel, her presence commanded attention, exuding confidence and allure that drew me in like a moth to a flame. "Your little boy toy looks a little busy, do you want to play with me?"

A shiver ran down my spine as Ariel's voice purred in my ear, her words laced with mischief. My gaze flickered between her and Benji, who was now bound and helpless. A part of me wanted to resist Ariel's tempting offer, to rush to Benji's side. But another part of me, a darker part, yearned for the unknown thrill that Ariel promised. Caught between duty and desire, I hesitated for a moment before answering. "What do you have in mind?" I asked cautiously, my voice betraying a hint of curiosity. Ariel's lips curled into a seductive smile as she gestured toward a dimly lit corner of the room. "Come with me," she murmured, her voice dripping with allure. I found myself following Ariel down the hallway back into the main room. "Sit, right here." She said with a stern voice pointing to a single chair. "I just want to thank the host the only way I know how."

I sat down, and Ariel began to give me an intimate dance, a tease, a show just for me. Her eyes locked onto mine, they looked to be full with a mixture of mischief and hunger. She moved closer, her body mere inches away from mine, teasingly close but never quite touching. It was an exquisite torture, a dance between temptation and restraint.

I swallowed hard, my heart pounding in my chest, I reached out for her waist to see if she would sit in my lap. She swatted my hand away and said, "uh-uh, you can look but you can't touch. I'll touch you in a moment. You need to learn how to sit back and enjoy pleasure." She continued to tease and toy with me. I wasn't even thinking about Benji in the other room anymore.

She got on the ground on her knees, and pulled out a small vibrator that fit delicately in one of her hands. She did not even bother to take my bottoms off, nor did she pull them to the side. The vibrator sat on top of my panties, right where my clit was. My eyes widened at the sudden sensation, and I let out a small gasp, my breath hitching in my throat. The vibrations were intense, and I could feel my body beginning to respond to the pleasure. Her eyes locked onto mine, and I could see the mischievous glint in her gaze.

"Do you like that?" she asked, her voice low and sultry. "Yes," I managed to choke out, my breath coming in short, shivering gulps. "More, please."

She smirked, reaching up to adjust the speed of the vibrator, making it even more intense. I arched my back, my hips pushing forward in the chair involuntarily, craving for more contact. Her hand came down on my thigh, gently restraining me. "Not yet," she whispered, her breath warm against my ear.

The sensation was intense, yet exhilarating. I could feel the vibrations pulsating through my entire body, a wave of pleasure that threatened to consume me. I moaned loudly, unable to contain my reactions. Her eyes, intense, continued to stay locked onto mine, at least when I could manage eye contact. Her grin spread wide as she continued to increase the speed. At that moment, I forgot everything else that had happened that night. In that moment, it was just her and the exquisite pleasure she offered. She leaned down, her breath hot and her lips just a whisper away from mine. "So you really like that?" she said, her lips brushing against my ear. "I bet you do. I'm going to give you so much more, sweetheart. So much more."

The anticipation was almost too much to bear. My heart pounded in my chest as her lips brushed against my ear, sending shivers down my spine. I couldn't help but nod in response, my eyes only able to drift closed as the pleasure intensified.

Her fingers trailed down my thigh, leaving a trail of goose-bumps in their path. She adjusted the vibrator once more, sending waves of electrifying pleasure coursing through me. I moaned softly, my hips bucking involuntarily against the chair. It was as though I was completely at her mercy, at the whim of her every touch.

"You're so wet for me, aren't you?" she asked, her voice low and seductive.

I gasped, my eyes flying wide as I tried to protest, but I was unable to form a coherent response. Her voice was intoxicating, like a siren's song that swirled around me, pulling me in deeper. I wanted to beg for more, to submit entirely to her every desire, but I was lost in pleasure, completely non verbal, so close to orgasm.

She brought her lips to mine, kissing me softly at first, then more urgently as our passion grew. Her tongue danced with mine, as she continued to press the vibrator against me, both of us lost in the moment. I moaned into her mouth, my body writhing under her touch. She smiled against my lips, her eyes sparkling with mischievous delight. "You see, sweetheart?" she said, breaking our kiss. "You're not just enjoying the vibrator, but my touch as well."

Barely slipping my panties to the side, she slid in two fingers, still holding the vibrator on my clit above the lingerie. "I want to make you soak these panties so you can't wear them for the rest of the night." The sensation was indescribable, a perfect mix of pleasure and pain that left me panting for more. Her fingers moved expertly, stroking and tickling me in all the right places, while the vibrator continued its relentless pulsations.

My body now trembled with lust as she increased the speed of the vibrator. Her fingers moved faster too, matching the rhythm of the vibrator, sending waves of pleasure coursing through my body. I moaned loudly, unable to control myself any longer.

"Yes, yes," I cried out, my voice hoarse with passion. "Please, more."

My moans grew louder, more intense as she drove me to the edge. The anticipation was almost unbearable, yet I begged for more, craving the release that was so tantalizingly close.

She leaned closer again, her breath warm against my skin as she whispered, "Are you ready for it? Are you ready to explode?"

I could barely answer, my voice reduced to a whispered plea, "Yes, yes, don't hold back. Make me yours."

With a final, powerful thrust of her fingers, she pushed me over the edge and I felt the warm liquid gush out of me, soaking my panties, soaking the chair I was sitting in, and also soaking Ariel's hand.

"Oh, God," I murmured, my voice raw from the intensity of the experience. "I can't believe how good that felt."

Ariel smiled, her eyes lingering on me as she gently wiped the remnants of our shared moment from her hand. "You're a natural," she whispered, her breath still warm against my skin. "I'm going to go wash my hands and see what everyone else is getting into. Do you need anything?"

"Oh no, I'm good, I'm gonna take a minute and then go find my drink. Maybe grab some water and hydrate myself after squirting so much." I said. I came to my senses and went looking for Benji. He was exactly where I left him. Still in a blissful state of shibari.

"Okay so Noah tied my arms, and then you left, and then we did a different tie, and now I am going to have them tie my legs too, but I was waiting for you!" Benji said excitedly.

"Yea? For me? How come?"

"Well Noah is going to help me get on the bed, they said the leg ties I'm getting are called futo ties or something? Anyways, I want to be tied up and helpless on the bed and have you sit on my face."

I blinked, my mind trying to process the request. Was Benji serious? This was definitely not something we had ever discussed before. My heart raced, I wanted him to participate tonight more than anything but this was not how I expected anything to go. I glanced back at Ariel, who had returned from making her rounds and was watching us with a grin on her face. "Well, well," she chimed in, her voice teasing. "Looks like we have an eager volunteer. Are you up for round two Callie?"

The room seemed to buzz with anticipation as people paused their activities to catch snippets of our conversation. I felt the weight of their eyes on me, their curiosity practically tangible. Taking a deep breath, I locked eyes with Benji. "Are you sure about this?" Benji nodded enthusiastically, a mix of excitement and vulnerability shining in his eyes. "I trust you, and I want to explore new things together. What better day for this than kink day?"

Noah helped Benji onto the bed, pretty center on the mattress. He lay there with his hands over his head, wrists tied together in a knot I did not recognize. Noah began to work on his legs with a natural colored brown jute rope. They bent his knees slightly, so that the back of his thighs and back of his calves were squished together. The rope bound tightly around his bent leg, knots up the side making a ladder like pattern.

"How's that feel?" Noah asked while tugging at the ties.

"Good! Doesn't hurt, but I don't think that I can get out of this." Benji said.

"That's the point babe," I said with sass while taking my seat on his face as requested.

Noah's fingers grazed against Benji's skin, their touch both gentle and possessive. It seemed as if they were proud of their shibari work, and with each tug at the ties, Benji's body responded, muscles flexing beneath the restraints. A shiver ran through him as he tested the limits of his captivity, realizing truly that escape was no longer an option.

As I settled into my seat on his face, I felt a surge of exhilaration course through me. The power exchange between us had always been a source of arousal, but now it seemed to intensify. My heart raced as I allowed myself to fully embrace this dominating role. Benji's muffled moans resonated through my body, he was helpless below me as I grinded on his face. I was getting more pleasure from seeing him so submissive and helpless than I was from his tongue on my clit. It was exhilarating to know that I had complete control over him in this moment.

This was no mere role play or slightly kinky escapade; we had crossed over into a realm of pure and consuming submission. Noah's hands continued to tug at Benji's restraints, finding satisfaction in the sound of his whimpers as the rope dug in.

The room was filled with a mix of sounds: the soft moans and muffled cries of Benji, the rustle of the rope as Noah tightened the knots, and the gentle slap of my skin against Benji's face. It created a symphony of power, desire, and vulnerability. In that moment, I felt a shift within me, as if the lines between play and reality had blurred. The intensity of the experience had seeped into my consciousness, and I began to question the depth of my own desires. I wanted to put this man through the turmoil of sexual hell that he had put me through. I grinded into Benji's face, harder, determined to drown him with my juices. I was glad I was staying hydrated after I already squirted once earlier in the evening. I could feel the heat building between my legs and the desperation in Benji's noises as he begged for relief. But, I only tightened the grip of my thighs further.

RED FLAGS & ROSES

I couldn't help but marvel at the sight before me. The way his body was twisted so beautifully by Noah's artistic hands, the way his muscles strained against the ropes, the look of his tattoos underneath tightened rope, the way his little noises pleaded for mercy, it was all too much for me to bear. My own arousal only heightened, my orgasm edging closer with each passing second. With a gasp, I climaxed, the waves of pleasure crashing over me like a tidal wave. Benji's face was a blur beneath me, his breath muffled by my weight, but I knew that he could feel the intensity of my orgasm as it coursed through me, and I dripped down the sides of his face. As I came down from the peak, I gently lifted my thighs off, granting him relief.

I sat there on the bed just in utter shock of the events that had unfolded. I really did not think he was coming to my orgy for starters, and I really didn't think that he would participate if he did come to the orgy, and, if he DID participate I thought it was going to be some regular normal sex or he was going be the one to dominate me like usual. Every idea of how I thought tonight was going to go just completely went out the window.

Noah started to untie him to give him a breather. I was still just sitting next to him on the bed collecting my thoughts. Suddenly my friend Macy walked in the red room, she was always so good at being fashionably late. She had a look of surprise on her face as the last of the ropes came undone on Benji's arms. She hadn't seen him since the night I took him home from The Social and I definitely did not do a good job of keeping her up to date that he was still around, and coming to the orgy.

"Well, well, well," she led on, "what is it we have here? Mr. Tough wants to be a bottom? I've got just the thing for you."

She said as she pulled a wooden paddle out of her tote bag. She must've just gotten there, took a minute to assess the main room, and then came to see what was up in the red room. She still had her clothes on, her coat, and immediately she was dipping her toes into the fun of being a dominate woman to a traditionally dominate man. "C'mon, up on your knees for me." She said while taking off her coat and dropping it in the corner of the room. "Let's see that ass I wanna make it red, make it match your rope kisses."

I just sat there, continuously in shock, as this man became more and more submissive before my eyes. He did not even question Macy, he just accepted his position and bent over for her as she asked of him. Macy began to laugh, which only heightened my sense of disbelief. I couldn't help but chuckle myself at the absurdity of the situation unfolding before us. As Benji maintained himself on all fours, I couldn't help but feel a mixture of intrigue and unease. Noah stood nearby, observing the scene with a mixture of concern and amusement. We all knew all too well that Benji's reputation was anything but submissive, but something about tonight seemed to have shifted the dynamics within him. Macy walked over to Benji and with a confident smirk, she lowered his boxer briefs revealing his bare ass, and lifted up the paddle and aimed for his right cheek. He just laid there and took it.

Macy circled Benji after her first hit, her eyes locked onto his exposed skin as if searching for the perfect target. She removed her heels and slipped out of her dress, leaving her in a set of dark blue lacey lingerie, the color of which seemed to be a bold choice given the situation. As the paddle connected with Benji's bottom again, the sound echoed through the room, punctuating the surreal moment. Macy continued this ritual, alternating cheeks, leaving a warm glow on Benji's behind. The cracking sounds of the paddle alarmed people in the other room and they scurried in one by one to see the towns bad boy face down ass up covered in marks and bruises. I didn't even know who he was anymore tonight. He just laid there and took it and didn't even make a sound.

Macy, satisfied with the job, dropped the paddle and stepped back to admire her handiwork. Benji sank onto his heels, panting slightly. It was as if he'd just run a marathon, but instead of exhaustion, he looked... alive. "Wow, um, thank you?" He said.

"You're welcome baby, taking advantage of men is my expertise."

I left the red room, and ventured into the main room to grab some much needed water. Dalton met eyes with me, "Everything okay?"

"Oh yea, there is just some surprisingly intense kink going on in that room I needed a breather."

"Well I was about to head in there, a handful of us were actually that have been out here for a minute, catch you back in there when you catch your breath? Would love to play with you tonight some too."

And in that moment, the crowds shifted. I found myself sitting alone on the couch, sipping my water, reveling in what just happened. I also arguably just needed to catch my breath after having a few orgasms in a row. In a short while, I was feeling better and back on my feet, headed for the red room eager to see what shenanigans Benji was finding himself a part of now.

Upon entering the dark space, I saw a gaggle of bodies, Jake, Alejandra, Benji, Dalton, Ariel, all on the bed, kind of snuggling, kind of kissing, kind of playing by exploring bodies. I was shocked to see Ariel engaging in play with men, but she seemed happy and safe so I let it be and didn't say anything. Some of the couples were scattered across the back wall, watching, also kissing, and engaging in lite play. Benji seemed to be back into a dominant head space as his fingers were deep inside of Alejandra.

"Any room for me?" I said making space for myself sitting up at the corner of the bed. Benji was now going hard on fingering Alejandra. "Does this make up for me missing your birthday? Huh?" He said as he continued pummeling three fingers inside of her deep. Jake was behind her, spooning her almost, biting at her neck and pulled her hair assisting Benji to get her to relax and release. Chad was standing in the corner, still yet to participate in any manner, but it was comical to me that he was just bumbling around watching the festivities, which often included his best friend being vulnerable. However, Benji still had not gotten naked. He was tied up in his boxers and a black shirt, Macy had only lowered his briefs to spank him, he was still one of the only people covered at the orgy that was actively participating. Benji shifted his body to be in between Alejandra's legs, he kept at the motion of shoving three of his fingers deep inside of her. Her back arched, her toes curled, and there it was, a waterfall of squirt heading straight for Benji. Guess he was going to have to lose some of that clothing he was holding onto now after all.

Benji sat up with a look on his face of pleasure and success. He criss-crossed his arms at his waist to pull the now squirt soaked shirt off over his head. His long hair was falling out of the bun it had been in as his shirt went over his head falling down to his shoulders. A silver sparkly chain sat atop his tattooed chest that was previously hidden by the t-shirt. He looked so good. I wanted more of him, especially now that it seemed he was back to the basics of practicing a dominate role.

"Daddy?!" I said loudly, and almost like a question. Both Benji and Jake looked up at me. What a powerful feeling. "Oh, sorry, I wanted Benji's attention." I said crawling closer to the edge of the bed. "Daddy, I want more." I laid down, back on the mattress right at the foot of the bed, my legs dangled off the corner. Benji got on his knees on the ground before me, and placed himself between my legs. He didn't go straight to eating me out or teasing my clit as I had anticipated, instead, he started nibbling at my inner thighs, small bites with his teeth, just a graze, a sensory experience. But then, he chomped down swiftly. That would be a bruise tomorrow. I squirmed a little caught off guard, "Don't fight it my pet, or you'll get another one." Dominant Benji was back and I was shivering in excitement.

He went down on me for a few moments, Dalton watching while sitting next to me on the bed. Benji lifted his head up and looked at me, leaning his chin on the bruise he just left on my thigh. "You know, I'm kinda tired, I think I'm going to take a little break, Dalton, here, you take over what I was doing. He stood up quickly, grabbing his beer that was on the end table. He didn't venture far, he just stood at the foot of the bed looking down at me enjoying the pleasures of Dalton's tongue and fingers tantalizing my pussy when he took over. I shifted my sight from Benji to Dalton, my eyes looking straight down through my legs as if I was looking down the barrel of a loaded gun, my soon to come orgasm being the bullet.

I was focused on what Dalton was doing to me like it was intricate spell work, but I was quickly distracted by a hand at my throat. Benji lifted my head up, forcing me to look at him. He spit on my face, didn't even ask me to open my mouth, and then open handedly served a smack to my right cheek. "I'm your fucking Daddy, not him. You look at ME when you cum. He's only going down on you right now because I told him too. You're still under my control."

Dalton paused for a moment, watching as Benji dominated me, but he eagerly continued to work on my sensitive folds. I could feel the warmth of the room and the pounding of my heart, my breaths becoming shallow as I anticipated what was to come. Benji, still holding my head in his hand, grunted and shoved two fingers deep into my mouth, causing me to choke on them. He smirked and patted me on the head, his voice heavy with authority. "Good girl. Now, let's see how well you take to your new lesson. You're going to ask to cum."

Benji had a cruel smile on his face as he watched Dalton and I. His hand still gripped my throat, a constant reminder that he was in control. I tried to meet his eyes, but my pleasure-drunk state made it difficult to focus. Benji kept lifting my head and slapping me every time I struggled to make eye contact with him. I could feel Dalton's fingers slipping inside me, his fingers pressing against my G-spot as he sucked on my clit. The sensation was intense, overwhelming, and I knew that it wouldn't be long before I reached the breaking point.

Benji lowered his lips to my ear and whispered sinfully, "Ask me, beg me for your orgasm. Show me your submission." The weight of his words, the commanding tone, it was almost too much to bear. A part of me longed to defy him, to resist his control, but another part ached to surrender, to give him what he demanded. I continued to squirm beneath Dalton's expert touch, my body trembling as I felt the orgasm building within me, threatening to break free.

"Please, Benji," I choked out, my voice hoarse from Benji's relentless dominance. "May I, may I cum?"

"Yes, yes you may my pet. You've been such a good girl." Benji released my throat and nodded to Dalton with a wicked grin, who then increased his pace. His fingers delved deeper within me, hitting my sweet spot with every thrust. The pleasure was intense, a mixture of pain and pleasure overwhelming my senses. I let out a whimper as the orgasm built up, each pulse in my clit sending a jolt up to my core.

I felt like I was floating on a cloud, suspended in a realm where pleasure and pain coexisted. As the climax came and left my body, I found myself longing for Benji's touch, even as he held me captive. There was a strange comfort in his dominance, a twisted sense of security in his cruelty. Chad approached Benji almost as soon as the scene was complete, blocking me from getting my aftercare from him. But Jake on the bed had watched the whole show and came to my rescue holding me as I gained my senses back.

"Hey man, I think I'm gonna head out of here soon, it's getting late, are you going to ride back home with me? Chad asked.

"Nah you can head out without me I think I'm going to stick around here and stay with Callie." he said as he climbed down on the bed, motioning to Jake to let go of me and offering to hold me in his arms instead. The next moments went by in a blur. I think truly I dozed off in the safety of Benji's touch. As the world spun around me, I couldn't help but feel a sense of relief wash over me. Benji's arms felt like a comforting embrace, shielding me from the chaos that had just unfolded. Jake gave me a warm smile, his eyes filled with understanding and concern. It was then that I realized how much I needed this moment of connection. Both of my boys, my Daddy's taking care of me.

Part Three

As the room slowly emptied, I allowed myself to sink deeper into the warmth of Benji's embrace. The dimly lit space around us was a testament to the intensity of our encounter. With each soft breath he took, I felt myself relaxing, the weight of the evening fading away. I started to come out of subspace, and got up off the bed, my legs only slightly shaky like a newborn baby deer. "I just wanna go grab some more water," I said heading out of the red room. Benji was quick behind me, holding my hand in his. Upon entering the main room, it was noticeable that people had left, and the night was coming to an end.

"Sorry Chad left in kind of a hurry? You know you can stay here, I have clean sheets and blankets for the red room," I said at Benji.

"Yea, for sure, I can help you tidy up and put clean sheets on. Everyone seems to be heading out, do you want to just go lay down with me?"

It was 3:30 in the morning, it was absolutely time to go lay down. We headed back down the hall, I stopped at the linen closet to grab fresh sheets. Benji ripped off the soiled ones and the waterproof mattress protector, and helped me lay the clean ones down. We turned off the lights and laid down next to each other, a slight amount of light coming in from the moon.

"Hey, you didn't get to cum tonight? Did you want to have sex before we head off to sleep?" I suggested now that it was just the two of us.

Benji turned to face me, his eyes glinting in the moonlight. "I was hoping you'd ask." I grinned, rolling onto my side to face him. "Are you sure? I don't want to pressure you or anything." He shook his head. "No, I'm sure. I've been wanting to do this all night." We moved closer, our bodies touching as we kissed. Our hands roamed over each other's skin, exploring every curve and contour. The anticipation and excitement was palpable, and I could feel desire coursing through my veins. I reached down, lowering his briefs that were shockingly still on him, sliding them off, revealing his already erect cock. I ran my hand along its length, watching as his eyes rolled back in pleasure. I knew what I wanted to do next. I positioned myself in between his legs and started to kiss at his thighs to tease him just as he had done with me all night.

Carefully, I traced my tongue along the inside of his thigh, feeling his muscles tense with anticipation as I slid lower and lower. Finally, I reached his hot, throbbing member, and I could feel him shiver with delight. I wrapped my lips around the tip and sucked gently, eliciting a soft moan from him. He was breathing heavily now, his hands gripping my hair as a silent plea for more.

I wanted to make this moment last as long as possible, so I alternated between sucking on his cock and gently stroking it. I could hear his ragged breathing getting faster and faster, and I knew that soon he would reach his breaking point.

His thighs quivered under my touch, and I knew I had found the right spot. I took a deep breath, inhaling the musky scent of his arousal. Benji moaned softly, encouraging me to continue.

With every tantalizing touch and lick, his breathing became more labored, and his moans grew louder. I could feel his desire building up inside him.

"Callie, fuck, I- please Callie, hold on, wait!" He said before pulling my hair to pull me off of pleasuring his cock. He looked like he saw a ghost. Flush in the face. "I just, you're probably the only person I could trust to explore this with...would you... consider eating my ass and maybe putting a finger or toy up there?"

I was taken aback by his request, but I could sense that he was genuinely expressing a vulnerability I had never seen before. He was being extremely submissive earlier in the evening. With a deep breath, I acknowledged that this was something we could explore together, and I slowly pulled away from his cock to gather my thoughts.

"Are you sure about this, Benji?" I whispered, my fingers tenderly brushing along his balls. "This is a big thing and I want to make sure you're completely comfortable with it." He nodded, his eyes locked onto mine.

"I trust you, Callie. You've always been the one to make me feel safe and open to new experiences. Please, I need you to do this for me. Tonight just feels like the night to try everything." With his words echoing in my mind, I positioned myself between his legs once more.

I took a steadying breath, my hands trembling slightly. This was not new territory for me, but it was a lot of pressure being someone's first for anything. I wanted to give Benji the experience he desired, to show him that he could feel safe and comfortable with me no matter what. I reached for the lube on the bedside table and squirted a generous amount into my hand. I could see Benji watching me intently, his eyes locked onto mine. With a deep breath, I gently parted his cheeks, exposing his backside to me. I took my fingers and slowly began to explore the sensitive skin around his entrance, ghosting my fingers along the sensitive nerves. Benji let out a soft whimper, his breathing continued to sound very ragged. I gave gentle kisses on the sensitive skin around his anus, I felt the muscles tighten and relax as I worked my tongue around his hole.

I slowly coated my fingers with more lube, spreading it around his entrance, my touch feather-like as I prepared him for what was to come. Benji let out a soft sigh, as I slid my finger inside of him, feeling him relax even more. I continued to explore his backside with my fingers, massaging and probing until he was ready for more. The anticipation was heavy as I reached for a small vibrating dildo from the bedside table. I switched it on and gently applied it to his hole. Benji let out a moan, his muscles clenching and releasing with each pulse, eager for more. I slowly inserted the toy, watching as his face contorted with pleasure and vulnerability. As I continued to pleasure him with the toy, I leaned in to kiss him, our tongues dancing together in warm embrace.

His moans grew louder with each gentle probing, his body arching into my touch. I reached for the lube again, pouring a generous amount into my hand. I slowly massaged it into my fingers, ensuring that they were well lubricated. With a dildo in one hand, slowly entering his hole in and out, I grabbed his cock in my other wet lubed hand and began to work it. Benji let out a soft gasp as I pleasured both his cock and hole at the same time. I could feel his body respond to my touch. He arched up into my hands, his hips bucking with each stroke. I gently continued to guide the dildo inside him, feeling him tense up. "That's it, Benji," I whispered, my voice low and sultry. "Take it all, let me show you how good this can feel." Benji's eyes locked onto mine, his expression a mix of surprise and pleasure. He pushed back against the dildo, his body bending to accept it. I could see the veins on his neck tense through his tattoos, his eyes fluttering with passion.

"Oh fuck, Callie," he groaned, his voice vibrating with emotion. "You really know how to make me feel good." I smiled, feeling a rush of pride and desire. It wasn't like I didn't know my way around toys being in a queer relationship with Alejandra, and Jake also for that matter.

I slowly increased the intensity of my strokes, feeling his body respond to my every touch. His moans became louder and more desperate, his hips bucking against my hand. I could see his breath quickening, his eyes locked onto mine.

I knew we were close to the edge, to that moment where everything would come together. With a deep breath, I reached for the lube once again, coating my fingers in it, and slowly began to massage his perineum.

Benji let out a sharp gasp, his body tensing up with every circle of my fingers, his breath coming faster and harder with each touch. His eyes locked onto mine, a desperate plea for more. I leaned in closer, my breath hot against his skin, and whispered, "You're so close." Benji's body shook with anticipation. His moans grew louder with each touch, his hips bucking harder and harder against my hand, the dildo still moving in and out of him in a steady rhythm. I could feel the tension building, the moment of release edging closer with each passing second. And then it happened. Benji let out a primal scream, his body shuddering violently as waves of pleasure washed over him. His eyelids fluttered, and he collapsed against the bed, spent.

We lay there together for a few moments, basking in the afterglow of our intimate moment. I could feel the weight of his body against mine, our hearts beating in unison, connected in a way that only we understood. Tonight it seemed to come together that he was the yin to my yang. My perfect switch in response to my switch energy. He could dish out what he could take and vis versa. This cat and mouse sexual game was a game neither of us could lose.

I nuzzled up to him, the sun slowly rising outside of the window, and I began to drift off to sleep. Our intense passion had ignited a flame that burned brighter with every stolen moment. As I traced my fingers lightly over his chest, I marveled at the way his body responded to my touch. It was a symphony of sensations – a harmonious dance of pleasure and surrender. From that fateful encounter at a crowded bar to this intimate sanctuary we shared, we had grown together, exploring the depths of our desires and unraveling layers of vulnerability. Our desires intertwined like vines, each longing perfectly mirrored by the other.

Chapter 8: 10/7

I fluttered my eyes open, what time was it? The red room was bright, my head was pounding, and Benji was still snoring next to me. The red room was extra warm feeling in the day time, the sun against the red velvet curtains. I rummaged for my phone to check the time. It was one in the afternoon and my phone was at 11% battery.

"Benji" I whispered shaking him gently at his shoulders. "Benji wake up!" His eyes opened and immediately revealed a familiar spark of mischief.

"Mm, good morning Callie," he grinned while stretching his arms high above his head. "Last night was something else. I'm still in shock every time I wake up in this room, this place is like something out of a movie."

"It's one in the afternoon, not morning, but yea" I chuckled. I don't even know why I woke him up. I didn't have anything to do, neither did he, I didn't need him to leave either. Looking through my phone despite it's low battery, I had a dozen texts from guests thanking me for letting them come to an orgy last night. I also discovered a few photos, a picture of Jake sitting so regal in his plush red robe, a picture of Alejandra hugging Ariel's ass looking drunk in love, and a picture of Benji all tied up in rope. I couldn't help but chuckle as I scrolled through the photos on my phone. The memories of last night's party flooded back, each image capturing a different moment of madness and revelry. It was a night to remember, that's for sure.

"Hey, look at these," I said, nudging Benji with my elbow. He groaned and rubbed his eyes, trying to shake off the remnants of sleep.

"You really know how to throw a party, Callie." I blushed at his compliment, feeling a warm sense of pride welling up inside me. Planning events like these had always been a passion of mine, and it seemed like I had found my calling in creating unforgettable experiences for people. "You know you've given me so many firsts, I don't know if I told you but you gave me my first threesome that one night with Alejandra. I have never had group sex until you came along with your whole wild world to introduce me to."

"Yea I remember you telling me that!" Man, I really did just kinda turn this man out. He was already so cool, but here I was just making him cooler by handing him once in a lifetime experiences on a silver platter. I sat there and thought about how he would share the stories of our adventures to his friends.

"I guess I'm just trying to say thanks Callie, for everything."

"Yea of course, I mean, I like you a lot, I like being able to have you around apart of everything. I hope you keep coming around. Our Halloween party is in a few weeks, you should definitely come to that!"

"I would love too but this month is really busy for me, besides Halloween week I'll be out of state on a work trip. That sounds like it'll be a good time though, I wish I didn't have to miss it!"

My brain was rattling with bad idea's of pushing the party a whole week forward just so he could come but that was insane and I wasn't going to actually do that. But damn was it upsetting that he wasn't going to be able to come.

"Okay well, we're hosting a Friendsgiving party a few weeks after Halloween so maybe you can make it to that!"

"Yea Callie, maybe, I don't know, we'll see" his voice seemed annoyed and almost defeated. "Just, remember, we're not dating. I just want to keep doing this, if you're catching feelings though, like real feelings, we can put a pause on things or just be friends. I don't want you coming at me saying I lead you on."

"No I know," I said bad quickly while lying through my teeth, "everything is good on my end, I just like having you around." I didn't know how to react to his statement about still not wanting to be in a relationship. I knew he was a casual fling, he's said since the beginning that this was all just casual, but I couldn't help but feel a pang of disappointment. Maybe it was my imagination, but I felt like he was drifting away during this conversation. I needed to get a grip on my emotions and not let them get the best of me.

Benji nodded, a small smile playing on his lips. "That's right, Callie. We're just friends having a good time. And hey, if you want to hook up again soon, just give me a call, alright?" He kicked his legs up and over the bed, pulling his pants on. "I'm gonna call an Uber and get out of here okay?"

The words "just friends" echoed in my head as I watched Benji dress. It was true, we were just friends. But there was something about him that made me feel something more. Something I couldn't quite put my finger on. I wished Benji a good day as he left, promising to call him if I wanted to hook up again. But as the door closed behind him, I couldn't help but feel like a piece of my heart had been torn from my chest and taken with him. I realized that I had developed stronger feelings for Benji than I had ever anticipated. What started as a casual friendship one night stand scenario had slowly evolved into something more, at least one sided. Now that his departure was imminent, and our situationship seemed to have an expiration date, I couldn't help but feel a deep sense of despair. Last night felt like the peak and it was going to be all downhill from here.

I couldn't let my emotions consume me. I had to be strong, to accept the reality of our "just friends" arrangement. After all, it was my own fault for allowing my heart to wander where it didn't belong. The more I tried to convince myself of this, the more I realized that denying my feelings wouldn't make them disappear.

The memories of our time together flooded my mind. The stolen glances, the lingering touches, and the late-night conversations that left me wanting more. How had I let myself fall so deeply into this labyrinth of emotions? It was as if I had unknowingly unlocked a door to a hidden chamber within my heart, revealing a realm I had never explored before.

I found myself pacing around the room, unable to shake off the ache that settled within my chest. The weight of wanting more with Benji hung heavily in the air, taunting me with how unattainable that dream was now. I closed my eyes, desperately trying to regain control over the whirlwind of emotions threatening to engulf me. The realization that our connection was destined to remain in the realm of nothing more than friends hit me with a force I had never anticipated. Perhaps it was a cruel twist of fate that we had been brought together only to realize our paths weren't supposed to align.

Chapter 9: 10/28

As the moon cast an eerie glow over the neighborhood, laughter and chatter filled the air. Tonight was the Halloween party that the throuple was hosting. Nearly 60 of our friends and other members of the polycule were coming.

The morning was spent vacuuming, prepping cocktail mixers, hanging up decorations, setting up the beer pong table, and making sure the costumes were just right. Thankfully Alejandra and Jake both were home to help me all day. The three of us were dressing up as the three blind mice. Alejandra wore a sexy little school girl skirt that was all white, and a cotton shirt crop top. We convinced Jake to wear a body-con white dress from our closet to match us. I was wearing borderline bridal lingerie showing the most skin out of the three of us. We all matched with mouse ear headbands and the tiny little beady black glasses. Dressing up as a throuple was already too much fun, getting Jake to wear more feminine clothing made it even better. Maybe next year we could get him to do The Powerpuff Girls with us.

It was 7 o'clock and the doorbell rang to the first couple of guests entering our home, and the party went off early. I adjusted my mouse ears while walking up to open the door. Within a short two hours I was surrounded by an incredible array of costumes. Our friend group never skimped out on an opportunity to dress up and go all out. Everyone that had showed up, dressed up, which was exciting but I just couldn't be 100% happy. It didn't matter how many people showed up, I wasn't going to have the best time because all I wanted was Benji to be here. It's just so upsetting that he couldn't come. I had become overwhelmingly distracted by him over the last two weeks. We had an incredible night with lots of intimate bonding at the orgy, and then he just became so busy with his work he couldn't even text a girl back. I went to grab another glass of punch, I needed to be drunker to stop spiraling while thinking about him.

My phone vibrated in my hand, I was glued to it hoping Benji would text me, that and i didn't have pockets in my sultry lingerie that I called a costume. Looking down at my phone seeing Benji's name flash on the screen, I was shocked. Our conversations had been very minimal over the last two weeks and I was feeling very friend zoned. I read the text he sent with both excitement and longing. "Hope you're having a good time at your party, wish I could've been there! Say hi to everyone for me!"

At least he thought me I guess. "I wish you could be here too, it's not the same without you" I admitted in a reply text, maybe that was a little too honest, maybe the alcohol is catching up with me as quickly as I was drinking it. My gaze wandered over the crowd, my smile faltering with anxiety. I twirled a strand of my hair, my heart tugging waiting on a text back. It was so hard to have a good time when all I wanted was him and I was left so open-ended.

Amidst the revelry of the party, my mind kept drifting back to moments with Benji, the last encounter we had that seemed to grow into something deeper. I kept glancing at my phone, realizing how much I missed his presence. He read my message but had not texted back. Maybe admitting I missed him was a little too much. With liquid confidence I decided to FaceTime him. Fuck it, whats the worst that could happen? I wanted him and I wanted him to know I wanted him. The lack of our texting conversations lately was weighing heavy on my soul. I needed to just call him. Copious amounts of alcohol was clouding my judgment and I was determined to prove myself to him at every available opportunity.

Anxiety slipping less and less over the course of the night as I drank more and more, but still clearly hanging on a tad bit when it came to Benji. I dint want to fuck anything up. Also he was at work and with friends and coworkers that didn't know about me. Calling him would be crazy right? I dialed the FaceTime anyways, hands trembling, was this too much? Am I being overbearing? I didn't even text him beforehand to say I wanted to call...right as I was certain it was a bad idea to call him, about to hang up, he answered. A mix of excitement and regret surged within me.

"Hey, Callie," Benji greeted, he was dimly lit just by the screen of his phone in the back of a car, presumably getting a ride back to the hotel from working at the convention all day that he was out of town for.

"Hey, Benji!" I held my phone aloft, the vibrant chaos of the party scene visible behind me for him to see. "Wish you were here, everyone misses you and wants to say hi!" a white lie, but I wanted him to feel like this was home, a place he'd come back to after his trip and just belong.

Benji leaned back against the seat, even through a phone screen I could tell he was looking me up and down as he

113

observed my sexy costume and the festivities behind me. "I know, me too. I really wish I could have gotten out of this trip. Oh really? Is that why you called?"

Someone handed me a shot. Holding my phone in one hand and a shot in the other I said, "yea, like everyone is asking where you are, we're all so sad you're not here but me the most!" I slammed the shot down my throat really fast.

"Hey! Everyone!" …oh no what was I doing. I then lifted my phone high to the couple of dozen friends in the room and shouted loudly enough to startle the crowd. "HEY EVERYONE! Sorry! Excuse me!! My Daddy is on the phone and he's sad he couldn't make it to the party to have fun and play, he's really feeling like he's missing out, I want everyone to say hi Daddy!! Okay? On three, one, two, three!"

The party guests followed the cheeky demand, "HIIIII DAD-DYYYY" in a loud group singing songy shout. Benji's eyes lit up. His smile was contagious, having me smile just as wide and I could feel my cheeks get as red as they do my after a few rounds of Benji slapping me in the face. Truly I loved worshiping him. The party guests quickly got over the distraction and went back to their own conversations.

"I really wish I could be there with you baby," Benji replied softly, "I wish I could teleport myself right away over there." Feeling drunkenly embarrassed I walked outside and away from the party to hear him better on the phone and chat with him for a few more moments. Wait a minute, did this man call me baby?

We shared some laughs about what all of our mutual friends dressed up as at the party. For a moment, the miles between us seemed to dissolve as we delved into conversation and shared some inside jokes, each minute strengthening the bond that had quietly woven itself between us.

While exchanging smiles through the screen, an idea of a silent understanding came passing between us despite the physical distance popped into my head. I kept anxiously twirling my hair some more, I knew I was giving eyes that reflected a blend of disappointment and affection, thankfully it was too dark for Benji to tell, especially through a phone screen.

My heart sank knowing the conversation was coming to an end. I needed to get back to my party, after all I was hosting. "I should head in. Long day tomorrow." Benji said on the other line as his Uber ride was ending and he needed to grab his things. "Yeah, go get some rest," I said with a reassuring smile. "Thanks for picking up. It feels better talking to you, even if it's just through the screen."

"Always," Benji replied, "Enjoy the rest of the party for me."

When the call ended my thoughts lingered on Benji's image on the screen. As I walked back into the house to the sounds of laughter and music from the party, I couldn't shake the feeling of just missing Benji. Yet, the brief FaceTime interaction had left me with a sense of warmth, the unspoken connection between felt strong even through some virtual exchanges.

As the night wore on, I found myself wandering away from the party, seeking solace in the quietude of the backyard. There were a few people scattered around a bonfire but it was much quieter and calm in comparison to the booming energy from inside of the house full of loud music and competitive beer pong. I got settled down on a camp chair around the fire, the chilly autumn breeze sending shivers down my spine. It made the hairs on my arms stand straight up. It was easy to think about how Benji just a few weeks before was kissing me up and down and making me react the same way. With a drunken sigh, I dialed Benji again, my heart racing at the thought of being too much. I hadn't had a drink in a while and I felt like I couldn't blame my impulse on alcohol this time.

"Hey, what's up?" Benji's voice echoed through the phone.

"Yeah, I just needed a breather, and I just can't stop thinking about you," my voice softer now. "It's not the same without you."

Complete silence lingered between us, filled with so much uncharted territory. I fumbled with my words, trying to articulate the tornado of emotions within me.

"Callie, I... I wish I could be there too," Benji murmured, his voice tinged with a hint of regret. "I miss being with you, but I'll be back soon. Enjoy your party."

The words hung in the air, suspended in the expanse of the night. My heart skipped a beat, I felt a connection beyond friendship, a bond that was being created out of thin air between me and Benji. But did he feel the same? It didn't seem like it. Maybe calling a second time was pushing it. "I miss you, Benji," I let out and confessed, my voice barely above a whisper. Quiet as a mouse, matching my Halloween costume.

More silence.

"You miss me? I'm just some guy. You have your partners there, enjoy your time at the party with them and your friends." Benji encouraged me, while not reciprocating any longing of missing me too.

With a heavy heart, I bid Benji goodnight to rejoin my friends and partners and the party, the pang of longing lingering even after he ended the call. My mind was filled with a newfound awareness of my feelings for Benji, feelings I never anticipated. I missed him. Fuck.

The festivities continued around me but here I was lost in thought, pondering the complexities of a connection. Benji was clear that he only wanted a casual relationship, but this was touching into situationship territory and my growing feelings were clouding my judgment. A quiet hope stirred within me, a hope that perhaps, someday, this might blossom into something more.

As the party wound down and guests bid their farewells, I lingered outside for a moment longer, staring at the moon. Its silvery glow hung in the night sky. A soft breeze rustled the leaves. Lost in my thoughts, I found solace in this moment of solitude.

I whispered into the night, my heart echoing the sentiment I couldn't voice earlier, "Maybe there's more to this than we realize, Benji." Would I manifest that to be true? Or would everything come crumbling down with feelings getting in the way.

Chapter 10: 11/6

Benji had just gotten home from his work trip, and to my surprise, he texted me signaling that he was home. "Hey Callie, just got back. Would love to catch up over dinner tomorrow night if you're free?" It felt like he suggested a date, and that was not the norm for our situationship. I felt a rush of nerves mixed with excitement at the thought of our reunion. This invitation had been unexpected, almost unbelievable. Benji, who's still keeping me at arm's length emotionally, had asked me out to dinner.

I stared at my phone screen, rereading Benji's text over and over again. The words seemed to dance before my eyes, like a secret invitation to a world I had only dreamt of. Dinner with him? Tomorrow night? It felt as though the universe had conspired to bring us closer, to bridge the emotional chasm that had always existed between us.

The time passed into the early evening, with a quick glance at the clock, I realized it was time to prepare for the night ahead. After a few moments of staring at the options of my closet, I settled on a simple yet elegant black dress that I knew accentuated my features just right. The dress hugged my curves in all the right places, the fabric smooth against my skin.

I fell upon my makeup collection, contemplating the right

look for the evening. I carefully lined my eyes with liquid ink, tracing a thin stroke along my lash line. I delicately picked up a palette of eye shadows adorned with an array of jewel-toned hues. With a steady hand and practiced precision, I swept the velvety pigment across my lids. The transformation was immediate; my eyes sparkled with newfound intensity.

With a final spritz of my favorite perfume, the scent being a combination of floral and fruity notes, I took one last look in the mirror. I added a finishing touch of a simple gold chain, and grabbed my phone, keys, and purse.

Glancing down at my phone before I shoved it in my purse, I noticed a message from Benji, confirming the time again. 7 o'clock at the Italian restaurant on the West side of town. A flutter of feelings was enveloping in my stomach at the thought of seeing him in just a short while.

Torn between excitement and apprehension, I took a deep breath and left for the restaurant, my mind swirling with unanswered questions and my heart full of selfish sexual desires.

The restaurant buzzed with activity, the subdued lighting casting a warm glow over the tables. Spotting Benji sitting at a corner booth, I couldn't help but notice how effortlessly he commanded attention, his confidence shining.

"Hey, stranger," he greeted me with a smirk, his eyes sparkling mischievously.

"Hey yourself," I replied, trying to mask the butterflies fluttering in my stomach.

We exchanged casual conversation, what is it with this man and casual. Tonight felt slightly different though, something secret not yet communicated hanging between us like a delicate thread waiting to unravel. Being out in public together wasn't something we really did. I still hadn't seem him since the morning after the orgy, other then those drunken FaceTime calls.

As the night persisted, he teased me mercilessly, his wit sharp and his laughter infectious. I was savoring every moment. "I'm surprised you asked me out," I blurted out, unable to contain the curiosity any longer.

Benji's expression shifted imperceptibly, a flicker of vulnerability flashing across his features before he masked it with a smirk. "Why, Callie, can't a guy take a friend out for dinner?"

Friend. There it was ringing in my ears. My hand sharply removed from his thigh almost involuntarily. His words stung, a reminder of the boundaries we'd carefully established. Yet, his eyes betrayed a different story, a complexity I couldn't decipher. I reached for a bread stick and shoved it in my mouth to keep myself from tearing up, we hadn't even ordered meals yet.

"So, Callie, it's great to finally catch up."

"Yep, indeed." I brushed him off.

We exchanged glances, Benji looked at me confused, our conversation halted momentarily as a waiter approached the table, breaking the tension.

"Good evening! Are you ready to order or do you need a few more minutes?

"I'll have the chicken parmigiana, please" Benji said quickly.

"Uh, yea I'll go with the penne arrabbiata. And a glass of your house white wine, please." I sputtered out knowing I'd need a whole bottle to calm my nerves tonight but a glass seemed more reasonable.

"Excellent choices. Chicken parmigiana, penne arrabbiata, and a glass of our house white wine. Anything else for now?

Benji responded, "Maybe just get us the bottle of the house

white, that's all. Thank you."

Thank fuck. I was planning on downing my first glass like a shot anyways. As the waiter departed, my frustration noticeably simmered.

"So... just friends, huh?"

"Yeah, I didn't want to give the wrong impression. You mean a lot to me, Callie, but I value our friendship too much to risk complicating things."

"I get it, I do. You've been clear about keeping things casual from the start, it's just... I thought maybe there was something more between us. At least I thought something was maybe progressing after a couple of months now of whatever this is. I guess I read it wrong."

"I'm sorry if I led you on. I didn't mean to."

Our eyes met, both clearly uncertain of what to say, the waiter dropping off our stemless wine glasses and full bottle.

"It's fine, really. Let's just enjoy our dinner." I said pouring my first glass of wine straight to the rim.

Dinner seemed ruined, what were we going to do, engage in small talk and attempt to mask the intensity of our unaddressed feelings? I was going to need to order something stronger than wine.

The night progressed, each moment charged with different confusing emotions, until the weight of the unspoken lingered too heavily in the air.

"Benji, why now?" I asked, my voice barely a whisper, laden with the weight of suppressed feelings. My head full of anxiety.

He hesitated, his gaze fixed on mine, a cluster of emotions clearly in his eyes. "I don't know, Callie. Maybe I just wanted to see you differently for once."

His words hung between us as I struggled with my emotions,

torn between the desire to delve deeper and the fear of shattering what fragile balance we'd maintained.

"I'm not looking for anything serious," he interjected, his voice firm.

"I know," I replied, a bittersweet ache settling in my chest, "But friends don't go out to fancy Italian restaurants and share a bottle of wine, can't you see how romantic this seems? This looks like a date Benji to everyone but you."

We lingered in silence, there was nothing else to say. The moment was awkward. The tension was so strong. As the meal wound down and the check arrived, I was more confused than ever and just wanted to go home.

Benji reached for the bill, "Let me take care of this, Callie."

But the gesture didn't sit right with me. Friends split bills, especially for a fancy dinner like this. My mind raced, thoughts colliding as I tried to decipher the evening's blurred lines.

"Benji, you really don't have to do that. We should split it," I insisted, "that's the friendly friend thing to do since this apparently isn't a date."

"Come on, it's my treat. Don't worry about it."

My inner turmoil intensified. I wanted to stand on the table and scream that friends didn't pay for romantic dinners, that this wasn't a casual outing between buddies.

"Pet, you're letting me pay for your meal and wine, you shut up, sit quiet and pretty, and let Daddy do something nice for you, okay?"

I sat there stunned. Turned on. Shocked. Just absolutely stunned. I had nothing to say. He placed his bank card in the receipt book, the waiter almost immediately came and grabbed it and brought it back. Benji signed the slip, dropped two twenty dollar bills on the table as a tip, and stood up.

"Well are you coming? Or are you just going to sit here all night?"

We drove to the restaurant separately and neither of us lived nearby. Did he have something else in mind? I stood up from my chair, and to my surprise he grabbed my faux fur coat off the back of my chair.

"C'mon let's go, I have plans for our night." he said in a dominating strong tone. He started heading out of the restaurant, still carrying my jacket. I walked behind him, his pace increasing as I tried to keep up with him almost as he was running away from me playing a game of sorts.

His pace picking up now in the parking lot, he headed for his car. "Benji c'mon and give me my jacket I parked over here!"

He turned and looked at me with mischief in his eyes. "Come and get it," he teased as he opened the back door to his sedan and tossed my jacket in. He stood there, his arm resting on the roof of his car, almost proud of his minor bullying. He was really pissing me off.

"What the fuck is your deal tonight? Is this how we're just going to end things? I like you, you don't wanna date me, so now you're just going to fucking bully me?" I leaned over into the backseat of his car and reached for my jacket that he tossed all the way to the other side.

"How could you get yourself stuck in this little predicament?" Benji said, now quickly pushing me to get fully in the backseat, slamming the door behind me. I turned over, grabbed at the door handle, the child locks were on. I was locked in. It all happened so quickly, before I knew it he was sitting in the driver seat, backing out of the parking space, and we were headed off out of the restaurant lot and down the road.

"Where are we going? What are you doing?"

123

"Sssh pet, you speak when you're spoken too."

He seemed playful, shockingly I trusted him, so I just sat down in the middle back seat and went along with whatever it was he was doing. We didn't drive far before he turned down a dirt road, and parked about another mile down. We were near one of the local falls, it was past nine o'clock at night, nobody was out here. Benji put the car in park, cracked all four windows an inch, turned off the engine, and looked back at me.

"So you don't like that I want to just be friends huh?" He said as he got out of the front seat, and closed the door behind him. Standing just outside of the driver side back seat window he took his shirt off and put it on the roof. "Well since we're not friends I don't have to play nice when I fuck you I guess," now taking off his belt, his boots, his pants, "I don't want to be more than friends, you seem to have an issue with just being friends, so how about we become less than friends tonight, shall we?" His voice was sultry and taunting.

He opened up the backseat door and crawled in after me, as I crawled away from him, my back up against the passenger side back door. His hands met my hips and he pulled me down, me now laying flat on my back across the whole back seat.

"We're not friends, you're just my hole, and tonight I'm going to use you."

He lifted up my black dress, and didn't even move my panties to the side, he gripped them tight with his right hand and ripped them right off. "Here, bite down on this, we don't want you making too much noise out here," shoving my own ripped wet panties in my mouth as a gag. "Good girl."

A fucked up part of me was just so excited for what was to come next. Benji's lips were close to my face, his eyes kept locking with mine. He went in for my neck and bit down hard.

124

My muffled screams of pain and pleasure coming from my gagged mouth. His right hand began to travel down my body, stopping at my clit and making circles over it. I moaned at his touch, and he moaned at noticing how wet I was. "So you DO want this," he said without question after feeling me.

I let out a well-needed moan as I took him halfway in, "Good girl. God, I love it when we get mad at each other." This WAS a game to him. Suddenly, Benji's hands were around my back, holding my hips up to him as if I was a lifeless doll. He began pounding deep inside of me, holding my hips up still, fucking me harder than he ever had before. My right hand dangled off the edge of the seat, gripping at the back of the leather seat in front of us, digging my nails in as deep as his dick is in me. "If you're a good hole for me, there's a reward in it for you."

His thrusts came faster and faster, Benji quickly approaching release. "Fuck I love using you, this is all you're good for you know that right?" Still unable to respond, my panties still in my mouth now even more sopping wet from my own saliva, dripping out of the corners of my mouth. He pounds me harder and harder and puts his whole left hand on my face, covering my mouth, my nose, uniquely keeping me from oxygen as he pummels me into the seat.

Squirming below him, fighting back at him putting all of his weight on me, he just holds me down harder. He removes his hand from my face and lets me catch my breath for just a moment before placing both of his hands around my neck, using his hands around my neck to balance himself on top of me as he keeps just thrusting into me with all the force he has. "You're doing so good for me pet," he says moments before spitting in my face. He releases his right dominant hand and slaps me across the face, the spit spraying in the air from the impact of his hand to my cheek.

Benji decides to take the gag out of my mouth, grabs me by the bangs, and forces my mouth onto his cock. "My car, my rules," he says as he slams into the back of my throat. One thrust, a second thrust, "Fuck I'm gonna cum," a third thrust, and suddenly his cock became putty in my mouth as his semen slid down the back of my throat. He continued to hold his cock in my mouth as he went soft, choking me and gagging me with his cum.

"You've been a good and useful slut for me, so as promised, here's your reward."

He pulls himself out of my mouth, flips me over the center console on my knees, and begins spanking me. "We're going to see how red this ass of yours can get. You withstand my torture, and I'll let you cum."

"FUCK!" I cry out as his bare hand spanks my left cheek.

"Look at you with your voice back, you be quiet or I'll gag you again," he spanks me again, only harder. I bite my tongue and take the pain in stride. "That's better," he says. He spanks me a few more times, evening out both cheeks with the same level of pain attention.

Suddenly he stops, "You've been so good for me, and alas, I'm a man of my word." He takes his thumb and begins rubbing harshly at my clit, "Yes, Benji, yes!" I cry out in pleasure, absolutely destroyed in subspace. He slips two fingers in me, still rubbing at my clit with his other hand. I'm enjoying every minute of his undivided attention to everywhere my body desires him. I went through so much pain and the reward was worth it. His head falls onto my back leaning into me as he continues fingering me harder and faster with his left hand, and rubbing my clit steadily with his right. His heaving breaths are warm on my skin, and suddenly it's upon me, crashing through like waves in a hurricane. I feel it course through my nipples and send shocks to my clit, every nerve ending in my body feels on fire. My eyes shut and mouth wide open, moaning his name, "Benji- fuck! God Daddy, yes, yes, YES DADDY FUCK, right there, ohhhh-" and I find myself squirting all over his back seat. His fault, thankfully for him his seats are leather.

He pulls me back and lays me in his lap on the backseat. He reaches for a perfectly placed single cigarette and lighter in the cubby of the door before opening the door next to him. He lights up his smoke and places the lighter beside him. His cigarette on his lips, he plays with my hair in his lap.

I find myself crying, laughing, and shaking all at once. "There there pet, you did so good for Daddy, let's get you cleaned up okay? Just relax, let's calm down first, catch your bearings." I caught myself dozing off in subspace in his lap, my dress still on, lifted up to my chest and stretched out.

When I came to my senses I was laying in the back seat alone, I realized, oh shit, we're moving. Benji was in the front seat driving, "You okay Princess? Subspace hit you really hard, I'm just trying to get you home."

"My, my car?" I stammered, sitting up now.

"You're in no condition to drive, I'll see if Jake or Alejandra can help me get it back to your house after I get you home. Don't worry."

I felt myself getting sleepy again, watching the light of the street lamps hit the car in a pattern. Like counting sheep, the lights made me tranquil in my submission. I laid back down, closed my eyes, and put my trust into Benji for the rest of the evening's journey.

Chapter 11: 11/17

The morning of Friendsgiving was upon us. Being in a polycule, a handful of us wouldn't see each other on the actual holiday so we wanted to celebrate early with the people that were closest to us all.

I busied myself in the kitchen, wrestling with the colossal sized turkey I bought, determined to conquer this centerpiece. I was quite the cook, but a 32 pound turkey was quite the challenge.

Jake, with his knack for mixology, concocted a signature cocktail that promised to be the perfect complement to our Thanksgiving spread. It sat nicely in a punch bowl on an empty table we usually used for beer pong, the table ready to be garnished with all the side dishes our friends committed to bringing.

Alejandra navigated the realm of deviled eggs in the kitchen beside me. Do you understand how many eggs you need for a Friendsgiving of 25 people? Her laughter filled the room, adding an extra layer of warmth to our bustling kitchen.

Our house hummed with the arrival of friends, each one bearing a dish to contribute to our communal feast. From stuffing to cranberry sauce, pumpkin pie to sweet potato casserole, the table began to look full of delicious holiday foods and treats.

Jake and Alejandra were slightly hoping that Benji wasn't going to show up despite being invited. After the antics he pulled with me last week they felt like he had an intoxicating hold of me that wasn't healthy.

As the clock ticked closer to the anticipated mealtime, the final preparations fell into place. The turkey emerged from the oven, its golden-brown skin glistening under the soft kitchen light—a triumph I couldn't help but beam proudly at.

"Is Benji coming?" Macy asked, "Yea is he coming?" Alejandra chimed in with an annoyance. My friends knew the general details of my situationship with him. I invited him to Friendsgiving but he never responded to the text. I didn't want to be pushy, so I assumed safely that he wasn't coming. I kept feeling like I was pushing him away from me with the ideas that I wanted more than the casual we agreed too.

"I don't know, he was invited but I haven't heard from him" I said, placing the turkey center on the table. "Are we ready to eat?"

With all of our friends and chosen family, our hearts brimming with thankfulness for the love, support, and companionship that enriched our lives, we all lined up with empty plates and empty stomachs to indulge in the group effort meal that was prepared. I found a spot on the couch between two friends and placed my plate in my lap.

As I settled onto the couch, a warm plate of delicious Friendsgiving delights balanced precariously on my lap, anticipation mingled with a familiar sense of contentment. The aromas of roasted turkey, cranberry sauce, and savory stuffing filled the air, promising a feast that transcended mere sustenance, a celebration of friendship, gratitude, and the cherished moments we shared.

The doorbell suddenly rang, an unwelcome intrusion in the midst of our intimate gathering. I glanced at the clock, eyebrows furrowing in confusion. Who could be arriving so late? "Maybe it's Benji showing up after all?" suggested Jake. It was probably just a package. I put my plate down on a tray table and scuffled down the stairs to check regardless. My heart skipped a beat as I realized Jake might be right. It might be Benji.

I had extended the invitation to him via text a week ago, assuming he wouldn't actually come, and he never responded. Our relationship, or whatever it was we had, hovered in the undefined space between friendship and something more, so it definitely felt like Friendsgiving was a little too intimate for him and I dare let myself dream too hard about him actually showing up. Yet, here he was, on the porch with a bouquet of flowers. "Hey sorry I'm late, I didn't have time to make anything but thought I'd bring these?"

"It's… it's okay. Thank you, um, come on in," I managed, my voice slightly strained, masking the turmoil of emotions swirling within me.

A dozen pairs of curious eyes followed me as I made my way back up the stairs, Benji behind me, his flowers in my hand.

I couldn't help but feel a knot tighten in my stomach. He'd been to parties before. But this was different, this was intimate. This felt like family. Also there was the added weight of Alejandra and Jake not being all too happy with him.

I placed the flowers on the table and made my way back to my chiseled out space on the couch, nervously eating my meal now as Benji navigated the room on his own, engaging in casual conversations, his charm effortlessly drawing people in.

Most of my friends were meeting him for the first time, their curious glances and whispers signaling their interest in this enigmatic figure who had finally graced us with his presence. The handful of people that already knew him met him previously at the orgy. The friends that didn't know him yet knew he went to the orgy. Everything was balanced and bound to break if any of my friends spilled my feelings for him. His laughter echoed through the space as he mingled with everyone.

As the night progressed, and the contents of our plates switched from savory side dishes to apple pie, I found myself stealing glances at Benji, observing the subtle nuances of his interactions. He seemed to effortlessly blend into the dynamic of our group, and nobody was spoiling my truths of love to him.

As the night approached, guests lingered, reluctant to bid their farewells, their laughter and chatter echoing in the dwindling hours of the evening, a bittersweet atmosphere settled over our gathering.

"You were a joy to meet, Benji," one of my friends remarked, their smiles genuine as they exchanged parting pleasantries.

"Yeah, thanks for coming, man. It was great meeting you, it's no wonder Callie likes you," another chimed in, a warmth in their tone that hinted at a budding friendship that formed over the course of the evening.

As the last of our guests bid their goodbyes, the room fell into a tranquil lull. Benji lingered, and he moved to help me clear the table, an unexpected gesture that caught me off guard. Jake was already working on some dishes and Alejandra was putting leftovers into Pyrex containers.

"Let me help you with this," Benji offered, rolling up his

sleeves as he began stacking dishes and bringing them into the kitchen.

As we worked in companionable silence, the clang of dishes punctuating the quietness, Benji's gaze lingered on me. His eyes held a silent question.

"Callie, I've been thinking," he began, breaking the comfortable silence that had settled between us.

My heart skipped a beat, a familiar rush of anticipation mingled with apprehension. I braced myself for the words that followed, words that might unravel the carefully constructed boundaries we had tiptoed around for so long.

"Tonight feels different. I'd like to stay if you're okay with that and talk."

His words hung in the air, heavy with implications that threatened to shake the delicate equilibrium we had maintained. I felt a whirlwind of conflicting emotions—surprise, apprehension, and a hint of longing.

Benji, the very person who had always been clear about keeping things casual, now stood before me, suggesting something that contradicted his previous stance. The hypocrisy was glaring, and yet, in that moment, I found myself wanting him to stay.

A myriad of thoughts raced through my mind—a carousel of doubts and desires, the unspoken hope that maybe tonight would be different, that maybe his presence here, now, was a testament to a shift in his feelings.

"Uh, yea, of course! I'd um, love that? That's just not at all what I expected you to ask."

Benji smiled, his eyes flickering with a mixture of relief and uncertainty. It was as if he had taken a leap of faith, unsure of the landing, but willing to risk it nonetheless. I couldn't help but feel a surge of warmth in my chest at the vulnerability he was showing. He stepped closer, bridging the gap between us, his hand reaching out to gently brush against mine. His touch sent shivers down my spine, awakening something deep within me that I had long suppressed.

The air crackled with an electric tension, and I found myself holding my breath, waiting for what would happen next. With a nervous laugh, Benji tucked a strand of hair behind my ear. "I know this might seem sudden, but lately, I've been thinking a lot about us," he admitted, his voice barely above a whisper.

"I know, I've never been one for sticking around," he admitted, his voice tinged with sincerity. "But tonight... I don't know. Something about being here with you feels different. Like maybe it's time to let go of old habits."

His words hung between us, suspended in the air like a delicate spider's web. I couldn't help but wonder what had sparked this change in him. Had he finally realized that his fear of commitment was holding him back from something meaningful?

"After the last time we saw each other, I just thought a lot about what you had to say about everything and realized my actions have not been matching my words."

I studied his face, searching for any hint of apprehension or doubt. Yet, all I found was an earnestness that seemed to come from somewhere deep within him. It was as if a veil had been lifted, revealing a side of him I had never seen before.

"Alright, um, well I gotta finish helping Jake and Alejandra with the cleanup but, you and I can stay in the red room tonight when this is done?"

"I'd like that a lot actually" He said in response.

We finished up the dishes, and I headed downstairs, Benji

following me, to grab another glass of wine.

"So I was thinking," Benji started, "can we talk for a minute?"

"Of course" I said as I nervously took a sip from my cup.

"I'm really confused, constantly, I know I said I didn't want anything, but Callie I don't know. Maybe it's the holiday spirit. But I feel like there's something here between us."

I felt a flutter in my stomach. "Benji, I…"

He interrupted gently, "I know I've been pushing this off saying I don't want anything serious, but I can change my mind right?"

I looked into Benji's eyes, searching for any hint of doubt or hesitation. The warmth in his gaze reassured me that he was being genuine, that his words were not mere empty promises. The flutter in my stomach grew stronger, a mix of excitement and uncertainty swirling within me. Taking a deep breath, I set my wine glass down and reached out to gently grasp Benji's hand. "Benji," I began, my voice soft but determined, "I've liked you as more than just a friend or fuck buddy since like day one. You're going to have to learn a lot about polyamory and how this is going to work, but I am willing if you are. You are also going to have to get in the good graces of my partners again."

He nodded before grabbing my face and kissing me. As Benji's lips met mine, a surge of electricity shot through my body. We pulled away, our foreheads resting against each other as we caught our breaths. His eyes sparkled with a blend of excitement and vulnerability, mirroring the emotions flooding within me. It was terrifying yet exhilarating to take this leap into the unknown, to redefine the boundaries of our connection.

"Thank you," I whispered, my voice filled with gratitude. "For being open to this, for wanting more."

I grabbed his hand and led him to the red room. I was so excited at the new developing emotions between us, but no matter what I ate too much turkey tonight and found myself sleepy and not horny. "Hey sorry, I think I am gonna pass out soon, morning sex maybe?" I suggested.

Benji's lips curled into a gentle smile. "Don't apologize, love. It's been a long day for both of us. I would love to just snuggle and sleep."

We sank into the plush mattress, the softness cradling our tired bodies. Benji wrapped his arms around me, pulling me close as he pressed a tender kiss against my forehead. I closed my eyes, feeling his steady heartbeat against my chest.

Chapter 12: 11/20

It had been a few days since Friendsgiving, a shocking turn of events of Benji coming over and being cute? We didn't even have sex that night, nor the morning after. He just stayed to help clean up, we snuggled a bit and truly just slept together, no funny business. It felt like that was the shift in our relationship of friends to lovers. Just casual to more serious. I was prepared to text him today and ask him to hang out and generally pry on what we were more, but I did find it odd that I hadn't heard from him at all over the last couple of days. It was the holiday week so maybe he was just busy. Thanksgiving just wasn't a big deal for me, my family wasn't around, Jake's family had other plans, and Alejandra was gone with her family so, I kinda forgot that a lot of our friends were busy this week.

I stared at my phone, contemplating whether or not I should reach out to Benji. My fingers hovered over the keyboard, uncertainty gripping my heart. Was I reading too much into this? Maybe he was just caught up with work or family obligations. Why couldn't he text me first? Maybe I should wait and see if he texts me first. As the minutes ticked by, my mind wandered back to the way his body pressed against mine as we slept side by side. It felt like a dream, and I couldn't bear the thought of it turning into a nightmare.

With a deep breath, I decided to send him a casual message. "Hey Benji! Hope you're having a great holiday week. Just wanted to see if you wanted to hang out sometime soon? No pressure, just thought it would be nice to catch up." As I hit the send button, a wave of nervous anticipation washed over me. Minutes turned to hours of anguish.

Trying to shake off my worries, I busied myself with mundane tasks, attempting to distract my racing mind. But every flicker of my phone's screen brought with it a glimmer of hope, only to extinguish it just as quickly. It was as if time itself had conspired to elongate these silent days and amplify my confusion.

Finally, unable to bear the uncertainty any longer, I decided to call him. Fuck it. I dialed Benji's number, my heart pounding with every ringing tone. The suspense was unbearable, and I needed answers. Had something changed between us? Anxiety clawed its way through my veins, leaving me feeling raw and exposed. After what felt like an eternity, the call went to voicemail. A lump formed in my throat as I left a hesitant message, attempting to sound nonchalant while inwardly begging for him to return my call. "Hey, Benji. It's me... Just wanted to check in and see if everything's okay. Give me a call when you can, alright? Take care."

The day turned into night, and the silence between us grew louder with each passing hour. Doubt crept into my mind like a persistent shadow, whispering insecurities and painting vivid scenarios of rejection. Had I read too much into our time together? Perhaps it had only meant something to me. Maybe he changed his mind, again.

As the moon hung high in the midnight sky, I found myself sitting in my dimly lit living room, engulfed in a sea of uncertainty. Alejandra and Jake were sound asleep but I just

137

couldn't relax myself to allow my body rest. The weight of unanswered questions pressed down upon me, suffocating my every thought. What if Benji had decided that our connection was nothing more than a fleeting moment? What if I had misinterpreted those stolen glances and tender gestures?

Finally, a ping from my phone that had Benji's name attached to it. My heart raced as I unlocked my phone, trembling with a mix of anticipation and apprehension. The screen displayed a text message from Benji. Relief washed over me, but it quickly dissipated as I read his words. "Hey, sorry for the silence. Things have been pretty hectic on my end. There's something important I need to talk to you about though, I'm seeing someone now, and we're practicing monogamy. Sorry to tell you like this but, we have to just be friends going forward."

The words on the screen blurred together, and I had to read them over and over again, hoping that somehow their meaning would change. But each time, the reality remained the same. Benji was seeing someone else. My heart sank, shattering into a million broken pieces. The pain swept through me like a storm, leaving me breathless and lost. A muffled sob escaped my lips as tears streamed down my face. It felt as though the ground beneath me had crumbled away, leaving me suspended in a void of heartache. How could this be happening? Just day's ago everything was fine, and now, it was all gone. I sat there in the darkness, the weight of the world crashing down upon me. The ache in my chest grew unbearable, each beat of my heart echoing the loss I felt.

How dare he lead me on, make me believe that there was something more between us? How could he just drop this bombshell on me without any warning? How dare he? How could Benji just drop this on me through a text message? After all we had shared, the connection we had built, he had the audacity to reduce it to a few lines on a screen. My tears turned to fury as I reread his message, each word fueling the flames of my anger.

The worst part was in a week I had scheduled to get tattooed by him. I wanted to support him, and genuinely I liked his work, but I also wanted to be marked by him. Was it going to be weird to get tattooed by him now after he practically broke up with me and left my heart pieces? If I canceled I didn't wanna argue him on getting my deposit back. Part of me was just so mad I didn't want anything to do with him, I just wanted to ignore it, let him keep the hundred dollars, and block him on everything.

Another fucked up part of my brain thought that if I sat down in his chair for hours that we'd be forced to talk and maybe I could fix things. After everything he put me through, he had to hear me out right? I just couldn't understand, after weeks with me and polyamory in his face how he could choose monogamy.

I had to tell myself that after everything, at least that emotionally unavailable man would remember me for the rest of his life. I was his first threesome, his first foursome with his own best friend at that, his first orgy which also included him being tied up for the first time, receiving impact play for the first time, and engaging in anal play for the first time ever. I ruined that mans life, or well, made it better depending on who asked and how you looked at it.

I just kept staring at my phone, feeling the weight of Benji's words heavy on my chest. My mind was racing, attempting to make sense of everything that had just happened. I exhaled slowly, trying to calm my pounding heart. This felt like a nightmare that I was going to wake up from any moment.

I sent him a text: "Hey Benji, it's okay. I understand. Just let me know if you want to talk about it later. I hope you're happy with your decision. I guess I'll say my goodbyes after my tattoo appointment next week, see ya then one more time."

A few hours passed, and I received no response. I was left with an eerie silence that hung in the air, a testament to the reality that things between us had changed forever. I tried to focus on the fact that I had Alejandra and Jake in the other room ready to love on me if I woke them up and told them the news. But every time I looked at my phone, I felt a pang of pain. I hated feeling this way. Breakups weren't any easier just because I practiced polyamory. It didn't matter that I had two other partners in the other room that loved me. Benji broke my fucking heart, and I was going to be a wreck about it for a while. He felt like my person, my perfect person.

Chapter 13: 12/2

The studio buzzed with the hum of tattoo machines and the scent of antiseptic. I laid on the worn leather massage bed, nerves twisting my stomach into knots. Benji, with his charcoal eyes and easy smile, strolled in, a mischievous glint in his gaze that made my heart flutter and sink simultaneously.

I can't believe I signed myself up to still show up to this appointment with Benji after he practically crushed my soul. I guess I also can't believe he was still down to tattoo me with how I reacted too. Maybe if he was smarter he would've broken the news to me after this appointment, but whatever, here we are now.

As he approached me though, it was like all my apprehension just dissipated. "Ready for this, Callie?" His voice, a mixture of warmth and teasing, sent a shiver down my spine. I nodded, trying to mask the turmoil inside me. I had been tattooed plenty of times before, but a tattoo from him? Being in the room with him for hours? I was more nervous than ever. I was just ready to be over with this, tattoo done and then likely to never see Benji again.

He prepared his equipment, his movements deliberate and practiced. As he approached me with the stencil, a soft brush of his fingers against my skin sent a wave of heat through me, conflicting with the agony of unrequited affection. He worked professionally and in silence, which was probably worse than talking about what happened. He peeled back the stencil paper and it revealed the intricate gothic design he was placing on my hip. He didn't ask if I was happy with the placement, he just finished setting up his machine and ink caps in silence and started working. The familiar buzz of the tattoo machine replacing the awkward silence that hung in the air.

"You know, some people squirm and squeal during tattoos. Are you going to be one of those?" His playful tone echoed in my ears.

"I'll try my best to stay still," I replied, forcing a smile. I don't know how or why he was still being playful with me.

The needle touched my skin, and I flinched involuntarily. Benji chuckled, his eyes fixed on his work, as if my physical discomfort amused him.

I clenched my fists, determined to prove that I could handle the pain. But with every stroke of the needle, it felt like he was etching his memory deeper into my skin. Each prick sent a surge of bittersweet pleasure coursing through me, intertwining with the lingering ache of longing.

"You're doing great," he remarked after some time, his voice too casual, too detached. He knew those words would get to my praise kink. I smiled, but didn't give him too much.

Time crawled by. With each stroke of the needle, I felt more vulnerable, exposed under his skilled hands. The pain was excruciating, not from the needle but from the unspoken ache in my chest. Benji's proximity was both a balm and a torment.

"Why so quiet, Callie? You're usually full of stories," he said, breaking the silence around hour three.

"Just trying to endure," I murmured, fighting to keep my

composure. "It's hard being around you, Benji," I confessed, my voice barely above a whisper. "Every word, every touch, it all brings back memories that I've tried so hard to bury. And yet, here I am, willingly offering myself up for more pain."

Benji put his machine down, "I meant to tell you," he said softly but sternly, "I made a mistake, that girl I was seeing, well, it immediately did not work out. She's not you. She want's monogamy, which is something I am realizing I don't want thanks to you, it just wouldn't work her and I."

His words hung heavy in the air, mingling with the silence since he had put the tattoo machine down on his work station. I looked up at him in disbelief with hope in my eyes. "You... you made a mistake?" I stammered, my voice barely audible. Benji nodded, his dark eyes filled with sincerity. "I messed up, Callie. I thought I couldn't do your lifestyle so I said I didn't want a relationship, and then I started talking to someone that wanted more of the same old monogamy, and I thought that's what I wanted, but the truth is, I can't. I can't do that again. You opened me up to so much."

I blinked up at him, my heart pounding in my chest. His words so casual hung heavy in the air, filling the studio with an intoxicating mix of hope and uncertainty. I searched his eyes, desperate for any sign that he meant what he said and this wasn't just some cruel joke.

A flicker of vulnerability crossed his face before he turned away, picking up the tattoo machine once more. His fingers trembled slightly as he adjusted the needle, and I knew then that this moment was just as significant for him as it was for me.

"You don't want monogamy?" I asked cautiously, my voice laced with both curiosity and cautious optimism.

Benji glanced at me, a wistful smile playing at the corners of his lips. "I thought I did," he admitted, his voice barely above a whisper. "But ever since you walked into my life, everything changed. I don't really know what I want now."

He went back to jamming his needle into my skin, casually like this intense conversation didn't just happen before our eyes.

Benji's fingers traced the contours of my skin, his touch lingering longer than necessary. I caught a glimmer of something more behind his eyes, a hidden tenderness he dared not reveal. Was it my imagination, or did his strokes become slower, deliberate, as if he wanted this moment to linger as much as I did?

"I've always admired your resilience," he mused, his voice softer, catching me off guard. My heart skipped a beat. Was this a hint of something more, a crack in his usual aloof facade? Or was I merely grasping at straws, desperately hoping for a sign of reciprocation?

Honestly I was annoyed. I was annoyed at how long this was taking, I was annoyed that it seemed as if he just played with my emotions while he figured his own shit out. I was staring at him trying to figure out what thoughts were going on behind those big beautiful eyes of his. I didn't realize how intently I was staring at him before he looked back at me, his eyebrows lifted.

"What?" I said back with an annoyance to my voice.

"Don't you fucking what me." He said with pure sass.

"I just did. What are you gonna do about it?" I said with even more annoyance to the tone of my voice, giving the sass right back to him.

"What am I going to do about it? I'm going to put you in

your fucking place." He said that as he slammed his machine down on his work station, and reached for my throat with his gloved hands. The black vinyl felt wet to the touch of my skin, likely cause to ink or green soap being on them. I couldn't find my words as my body shook with sensual excitement from the danger of this man. The intensity in his eyes was distinguishable, a mixture of desire and anger that sent a jolt straight to my core.

"What do you want from me?" I whispered hoarsely, my heart pounding in my chest.

His lips brushed against my ear, sending shivers down my spine. "I want you to know your place, my pet. I think we've been playing with each others emotions long enough. You know that I am in charge here. Now, let me finish this piece, and then you can have what you want for sitting so well for me."

As the tattoo neared completion, the weight of emotions suffocated me.

"Done," he announced, breaking the silent spell.

I gazed at the masterpiece on my skin, a stunning artwork that hid the tension within.

"Stay for a minute while I clean up, we can grab a drink or something afterwards, yea?" he said as he began taking apart his machine, and sanitizing his station. I sat on the massage table I had just been laying on for hours, figuring I'd be told to move when he needed to spray it down and pack it up. I couldn't help but fidget, my gaze darting between the floor and the mirror above me, where the newly inked masterpiece now shimmered in the soft light.

Finally, he spoke again, a hint of something in his voice. "So, what do you want for sitting so well for me?"

I swallowed hard, my throat dry from the anxiety and turbulence that had been building all day. "I... I don't know. I guess I..."

"Ssshh" he hushed me while walking closer to me, still staring at the new tattoo on my hip, and whispered, "I'm not done with you yet." He reached down and began lifting up his shirt, revealing a thick, leather belt that glinted in the light. My heart raced as I realized what was about to happen. The tension between us had been growing all day and now, as I sat there on the massage table, I could feel the anticipation building. I could feel the heat of his body as he stood close. "Are you sure you want this?" he asked, his voice low and seductive. I nodded, my throat dry. I loved to be dominated by this man who had captured my heart. He took the belt in his hand and ran it slowly over my skin, leaving a trail of intense sensation that made me gasp. He cracked his belt into me, leaving more marks on me than just a fresh tattoo.

He spoke in a low, seductive voice, "You know what's going to happen next, don't you?" I nodded as I turned to face him, my eyes locked onto his. "Good. Because I want you to remember this moment, and every time you look at this tattoo, I want you to remember how much you love me."

He pushed himself onto me on the massage table, I was almost crawling away from him until I couldn't go any further without falling off the table.

"So, we're just right back to doing this again huh?" I said, my voice shaking.

"Yea I guess if you're cool with that?" He said, like he didn't just torment me and play with me emotionally for weeks. If I'm cool with it? Ugh. He was so confusing. But I still wanted him, even if he was going to hurt me again, physically or emotionally.

Actually, I was hoping to be hurt physically again, right here, right now. I was in love with him, and I was willing to hold on for dear life until he was in love with me too.

"I'd do everything all over again for you."

About the Author

Dana Christine Hare is an emerging voice in the dark romance literary world, making their debut novel that promises to captivate readers. Dana juggles a career in modeling, photography, and owning a small business all under the alias of Sinnabunny. Living a polyamorous lifestyle, Dana shares their life with two nesting partners, their daughter, three cats, and a chihuahua. As a first-time author, Dana brings a fresh and authentic voice to their writing, infusing it with inspiration from their diverse personal experiences and insights gained from their varied roles.

You can connect with me on:
- ☍ https://www.allmylinks.com/Sinnabunny

Made in the USA
Columbia, SC
08 March 2024

32348784R00093